Totally Bound Publishing books by Nikki McCoy:

Everything That You Are
My Forever

Keepers of the Gods
Son of Death
Master of Wrath
Keepers of the Night
Slave to Chaos

Of Blood and Spirit
Crimson Mate

Of Blood and Spirit

CRIMSON MATE

NIKKI MCCOY

Crimson Mate
ISBN # 978-1-78430-195-8
©Copyright Nikki McCoy 2014
Cover Art by Posh Gosh ©Copyright August 2014
Interior text design by Claire Siemaszkiewicz
Totally Bound Publishing

Published in 2014 by Totally Bound Publishing, Newland House, The Point, Weaver Road, Lincoln, LN6 3QN, United Kingdom.

Totally Bound Publishing is an imprint of Total-E-Ntwined Limited.

CRIMSON MATE

Dedication

To all those who face insurmountable boundaries in life and love — never give up, and never lose faith that hope will see you through.

Chapter One

Manning stepped into the terminal from the portable walkway and took a moment to acclimatize. New scents of body odor and cologne assaulted him and the clamor of bustling life rang in his ears, but the floor was firm and steady beneath his boots. After the past six hours of confined air travel, that was all that mattered.

"Oh, sweet mother of solid ground, how I've missed you," Tailor blurted beside him.

"Here we go again," Cain grumbled.

Manning looked down at the prostrate form beside him. Tailor was doubled over and rubbing his cheek almost obscenely on the thin, checkered carpet. Passengers still filing from the plane behind them craned their necks to stare at the spectacle, giving the man a wide berth as though his behavior might be contagious.

With a sigh, Manning rolled his eyes as his friend continued to murmur sweet nothings to the floor. "Are you done yet?"

"Just give me one more second." Tailor caressed the carpet a little too fondly for Manning's peace of mind then stood to his full six foot three inches of height, rifling a hand through his long, golden hair. "Okay, I'm good."

Cain shook his head and, with his wide frame, began clearing a path through the throngs of people rushing around them. "Seriously, man, do you have to do that every time? You're a fucking bird. The sky is your natural habitat. What's wrong with you?" The words were muttered under his breath, too low for anyone but them to hear.

"It's unnatural to fly with a man-made set of wings. And you can't tell me you don't feel the same way."

Cain grunted but didn't comment further. Not even Manning could argue with Tailor's statement. Being separated from nature with no option but to endure cramped spaces more than thirty thousand feet above ground level for hours on end was more than a little unsettling. With earth-bound spirits, air travel was especially brutal on Manning and Cain, but they had no other alternative. For two months they'd been traveling with haste to every shifter community in the United States, and Manning was beginning to think going overseas was inevitable.

His feline bristled instantly at the idea, its rumbling contentment at being grounded dissipating in the face of its ire. Manning fought down his own frustration in an effort to calm his spirit. They both understood the time constraint they were under, but that didn't lessen the strain of the objective.

"Tailor, get the car. We'll meet you out front."

Tailor gave a nod then veered off toward the car rental station while Manning and Cain took the stairs down to the baggage claim area. After gathering their luggage, they walked outside to wait, grimacing at the cloying Sacramento heat that settled over them. Manning stifled a silent prayer that he would be able to return to the cool, welcoming shades of the forests surrounding his community after this. He didn't want to build up his hopes only to deal with the pang of disappointment if this trip turned out to be just another failed attempt at his goal.

After several minutes, a fire-engine red BMW convertible pulled up in front of them and Tailor jumped out of the driver's seat. He spread his arms wide and broke into a huge grin. "Beautiful, right?"

Manning and Cain shared a look between them.

"What? It was all they had left, I swear. Damn people preferring their modest, economical cars. I was lucky to get this one. You'll thank me later."

While Tailor jogged around the vehicle to put their bags in the trunk, Manning slid into the passenger seat and watched Cain stroll to the other side and barricade the driver's door with his body.

The big man held out his hand expectantly when Tailor came back. "Hand over the keys."

Tailor gaped then snapped his mouth shut. "I paid for this ride. There's no way I'm letting you drive it."

"You should've thought about that before you insisted on driving the last car. It's my turn now."

He voiced a string of expletives that drew more attention than his earlier ritual of supplication then got into the back seat and didn't quiet until Cain was navigating through lunch-hour traffic on the highway. Manning dialed through the radio stations absently and stared out at the sea of smog and overcrowded buildings through his window. He wondered with no little irritation how the hell the residents of the city didn't suffocate in their own prison of technology and concrete walls. What little nature that did exist had been manufactured as well. Sparsely constructed parks and golf courses were more a tribute to what had once been a fertile land than places meant for relaxation.

A loud harrumph to his left pulled his attention away from the window. Cain's gaze dipped to the radio console then met his again.

"Shit, sorry, man." Manning hit the power button, silencing the rap music that had been blaring from the speakers, and scrubbed a hand over his face. "Where are we going this time?"

Cain assessed him shrewdly before answering. "The community is about an hour east of here. We're meeting the Alpha's daughter at a café then following her to meet the rest of the pack."

"And when is our flight out of here scheduled?"

"One week from now."

Manning shook his head. "Make it sooner. I'll meet with the pack after I'm done discussing our plans with the Alpha and his Betas. Our business should be concluded in a few days. No unpacking this time. We're getting in and out. Clean and simple. Contact the communities in England and Africa, and let them know we'll be going there after we hit up Texas. Purchase the tickets before we leave here and see to it that Australia is the last stop on our trip overseas. If I recall correctly, the Alpha of the community there has eight daughters. I want to put off that nightmare for as long as possible."

The corners of Cain's mouth turned down in a disapproving frown. "Your father would be disappointed if he heard you talk like that about finding your mate."

Manning ground his teeth at the soft reprimand. His father was at home, in pain and awaiting a death he wouldn't take because his only son hadn't found a mate yet. Manning wanted nothing more than to focus on taking revenge for his mother's murder first then start a family later, but he couldn't, not before ensuring the continuance of his line. "There isn't time to make with the pleasantries and deal with the bullshit of convincing every unmated female I meet that she's not the lucky winner."

"And when you find her, how do you think she'll feel about being impregnated then left at home while her mate is gone for months at a time?"

"Are you saying I shouldn't seek justice on my mother's behalf?"

Cain's barrel chest heaved with a long sigh. "No. I'm saying your mother wouldn't have wanted you to sacrifice the joy of finding your mate for the sake of producing heirs and taking revenge. With the way you're going now, you might not even be able to convince your mate to bond with you. It can't be forced, you know."

Manning snorted. "I don't think I'll have a problem in that area. All the females I've met so far are practically fighting over the privilege to become the mate of the new *Jaes'din*." In truth, Cain was right, but Manning just couldn't see any other options than the one he was taking.

His mother's killers were still on the loose and the only information they'd been able to gather was that they were trancers and well trained. Her death reeked of a professional hit carried out on the order of their enemy's king, but Manning had to be sure. Shifters and trancers had held a relatively peaceful animosity toward each other for much of the past century. If the recent kidnappings and murder had been perpetrated by a group of rebels among the trancers and he took retaliation upon the entire race, he could start a war that could be just as devastating for his people as for their enemy.

In all honesty, he had to admit he probably would have struck at the heart of the trancers by now if his father hadn't effectively delayed that option by staying alive. His father should have already joined his mate in death, as all shifters chose to do when their mates passed away. However, he was still hanging on to see his only son mated and their house's line continued. Since Manning was the last living, direct descendent of the original shifter, his responsibility to grant his father's wish was imperative.

As much as he would rather give his full attention to finding the murderers, he needed an heir first in the event that he died during the war, and so his father could find peace.

"I don't mean to be such an asshole about all of this. If my mate is resistant at first, I'll give her time to adjust."

Cain lifted a single brow, causing Manning to bite back the rest of his cynical thoughts. "She's out there. The Mother wouldn't have allowed your mom to die without providing you with a mate to carry on your line. Your father has held out for two months now. He can hold on for a few more."

Manning knew his old man was just stubborn enough to do that, but each month was one more his father would have to deal with the pain of missing his mate. Manning raked a hand through his hair then went back to staring out of the window.

"I've got a good feeling about this place," Tailor spoke up from the back seat. "I saw a picture of the

Alpha's daughter we're about to meet. California just doesn't get any better than that. Blonde, blue eyes, with legs longer than a country mile and tan skin kissed by the sun. Her spirit has got to be a minx, or some kind of sexy kitten. She's perfect for you."

Manning and Cain both looked back at the man as though he'd lost his mind.

"I can pull over and throw him in the trunk," Cain offered. "Save ourselves the embarrassment."

"Make sure you drill holes in the lid. We might need him later."

"Fine," Tailor grumbled. "But if she doesn't turn out to be your mate, I get first dibs."

Manning shrugged. "Have at. Just make sure Cain changes our flight reservations to include space for a coffin. We'll need it after her father, the Alpha, gets done with you."

Tailor paled and sat back in his seat while Cain smirked at him in the rear-view mirror. Twenty minutes later, they parked at a strip of coffee houses and tourist shops, and got out. The Black Bean, where Tamara was supposed to meet them, was located at the end of the block. Of course, Tailor spotted her first. She was standing outside and looking around with an air of subtle authority. He slapped Manning on the back in enthusiasm as they took a moment to appraise her. Manning had to grudgingly agree that she was everything his friend had reported her to be.

Tamara's blonde hair was trimmed short, a sign of confidence among the females of his race, and her white suit was modest yet defining. The curve of her trim waist and the slim length of her legs were plain to see under the material that only left more to the imagination. When she turned and her blue eyes lit on them, she smiled seductively and tilted her head to the side, as though she was sizing them up.

Tailor had been right. She was perfect. But there was no… Wait. A hot breeze wafted over him, carrying a scent that slammed into his gut and made his heart race. It was sultry and sweet, like dark chocolate mixed with a hint of rain. Arousal and possession heated his blood as his spirit roared within. His feline vied for control as it rejoiced in the finding of his mate and all but demanded he stake his claim right then.

"Oh, fuck," Manning whispered.

"Fuck?" Tailor said beside him. "Fuck as in, 'Oh, sweet Mother, I've found my mate'? I knew it! Damn, I hate you. Lucky bastard."

"Manning?" Cain asked from his other side, but Manning couldn't answer. His breath was trapped in his throat and his lungs had forgotten their function.

It wasn't the woman, however, who was giving off the scent that had his body and spirit responding like a lit fuse, but rather the man standing behind her.

He was smaller than the average shifter, including many of the females. Blue jeans hung low on his narrow hips and his slight chest was covered by a baggy, long-sleeved shirt that was at odds with the sweltering heat of the day. Hair fell in long, black waves over his eyes, brushing his shoulders, and when he stopped and turned to look straight at Manning, it seemed as though time ceased to exist.

With his advanced senses, Manning could hear the soft gasp that slipped past his mate's full lips and see the whites around his widened, gray eyes. They were almost silver in the bright daylight, and there was a depth to them that mesmerized him. Desire swept through him and his cock filled to the point of pain as a small, pink tongue flitted out to moisten the man's parted lips. Manning's canines exploded from his gums and it was all he could do to clench his jaw and fist his hands to keep his claws from emerging.

Then everything changed in the next heartbeat.

The sharp odor of fear stung his nose and, before he could react, the man dropped his cup of coffee and bolted in the other direction, disappearing around the corner of the building. Manning's heart went into overdrive as he took off after his mate. Swarms of people he hadn't noticed before milled about and created obstacles he didn't have time for in his haste. The shouts of his *Ketai* rang out in the distance, but he didn't have time for them either.

When he pushed past Tamara, she snatched at his sleeve, trying to jerk him to a halt, but he shrugged her off. As he turned right down the next street, he saw his mate scramble into a metallic blue car that began to pull out into traffic. His feline screamed at him to run faster. To catch his mate at all costs, and he tried, but it wasn't enough. He chased after the car carrying his mate until it was no longer visible amid the profusion of others.

With lungs burning and sweat pouring down his skin, Manning sank to his knees on the sidewalk. He knelt there on the side of a crowded street in the middle of an overflowing city and knew what it was, for the first time in his life, to be utterly alone.

Desperately, he closed his eyes and recalled the vision of the man before his memory could lose it. The man had been unlike anything he'd ever envisioned in a mate. Each shifter was born with an animal spirit unique to them, but their general, physical characteristics were almost always the same — thick, strong bones, well-developed muscles, with golden skin and above-average height. His mate had lacked all of that, and yet, he'd been absolutely stunning.

His pale, chiseled features had been tinted with a faint flush in his cheeks and the hint of a shadow along his jaw. From the way his clothes had billowed behind his body while he fled, Manning could tell the man was slim, almost petite in comparison to nearly all but the adolescents of their race.

Was he still a child?

Manning hadn't garnered the impression of innocence in the man's expressive eyes, but it was a possibility he would have to take into consideration. A rough tug on his arm brought him back to his surroundings.

Cain stared down at him, a mixture of apprehension and confusion on his broad face. "Are you all right, *Jaes'din*?"

The use of his title brought him back to full awareness and he climbed slowly to his feet. Tailor now blocked the path his mate had taken but it didn't matter. The enormity of what he'd found and lost in the matter of a few moments sank in and he fought to keep his head above the tide of despair that threatened to drown him.

His feline hissed and spat its fury, but it was no longer at the loss of their mate. His spirit now seethed at the futility that was bleeding into his soul. Determinedly, he shoved the emotion from his heart, firmed his shoulders and turned to look at Tamara, who was standing behind him.

"That man, is he a member of your community?"

Her arched brows drew down in a frown. "The one you were chasing after? No. I've never seen him before. Do you know him?"

Manning stared again in the direction his mate had taken, setting his shoulders in firm resolve. "Not yet, but I will. Tailor, get the car and bring it around. We're going hunting."

* * * *

Quinn veered into the parking lot, narrowly missing one of the neighbor's vehicles, and brought his car to a screeching stop. After grabbing his backpack from the passenger seat, he ran in through the backdoor of the townhouse and locked it, then did the same with every window and the front door. Only when he was upstairs in his room, back to the wall, did he allow himself a moment to breathe, to think.

While he took in great gulps of air, Quinn tried to push down the fear that coursed through him and focus on calming exercises to force his erratic thoughts under control. His body was simply going through a natural reaction, a response to a man he'd found aesthetically pleasing. He did have hormones, after all, and just because he suppressed them didn't mean they didn't exist. He'd always known his arousal would flare sooner or later, as his sister was constantly reminding him. Control was not absolute. All he needed to do was figure out what it was about the man that had triggered his slip and avoid it at all costs.

The creature inside him didn't seem to think so, however. They were usually in sync with each other's instincts and emotions, but this time, the entity raged against his decision to run. Even now, it fought him for dominance and urged him to return to the café to seek out the mysterious stranger who had provoked a reaction out of him that he hadn't had in years.

What's wrong with you? You're supposed to be on my side. The creature responded by sending out a surge of lust that was nearly as strong as the tide that had hit Quinn when he'd seen the guy on the street. Quinn gasped, immediately tamping down his hormones, which caused the creature to howl and retreat within. *You know what they were. We can't risk it.* When there was no answer, he willed his trembling body to relax.

A quick glance down revealed the tent that was still going on in the crotch of his pants and he let loose a low groan. He unfastened the button and zipper, let the material fall to his ankles and winced as he lightly rapped his dick. When that didn't work, he squeezed his balls tightly and drew them down. Endorphins rushed through his blood as an image of the man he'd seen earlier popped into his mind. The slight pain only seemed to heighten his arousal and harden his cock further.

With a snarl of frustration, he divested himself of shoes and clothes then headed to the bathroom. Under the cold spray of the shower, he shivered and cursed until his erection finally deflated and the shaking in his hands was owing only to the drop in temperature. After he toweled himself dry, Quinn walked back to his bedroom and dressed in a different outfit. From his backpack, he withdrew his journal and sketchpad and sat on his bed. Though, instead of writing out his churning emotions to help him cope with them, he grabbed a pencil and began drawing out the scene that was etched in his mind.

Because of his photographic memory and excellent vision, he remembered every detail to perfection. Slowly, the image of the man came to life on the blank sheet of paper. Short, black hair trimmed neatly at the edges had topped winged brows and a straight nose slightly arched on the bridge. The top lip had been thinner than the bottom and his strong jaw had been cleanly shaven, showing a small scar that ran along the curve of it on the left side.

The man's chest had been broad and thick, and the muscles in his arms had rippled beneath smooth, tanned skin. Form-fitting jeans and a tight, white T-shirt had clearly displayed the long lines of his tall, well-built frame. Quinn made sure to include all of the minute faults he'd seen as well, such as the way the stranger's feet seemed overly large, and how one ear was lower than the other. The eyes were last, and he recalled all too well the large orbs that had appeared as black as the man's hair, yet deeper than the vastness of the night sky.

As Quinn started on the two men that had been standing on either side of the stranger, his fear gradually subsided. He'd instantly known all three were shifters, including the female who'd been standing outside of the shop, yet that fact hadn't bothered him at all. While it was easy for his kind to recognize their enemy by scent, shifters were unable to do the same. There was no way the men could've instantly identified him as a trancer.

And the country they were in was the unofficial territory of shifters, after all. The few trancers who chose to live in the United States and separate themselves from the politics of both races understood that their peace was contingent upon their ability to remain inconspicuous, which worked, for the most part. Any trancers who were caught were simply forced to vacate the country instead of put to death, so long as they didn't cause any trouble.

What bothered Quinn was his reaction to the dark, handsome shifter who now plagued his thoughts.

He'd become aroused, and not in any fashion that could even remotely be described as subtle. His unbidden desire had been stronger than anything he'd felt in the past. Stronger, even, than the time he'd discovered his arousal could incite uncontrollable wrath and lust in others. A violent shiver racked his body at the memory, but he shoved it to the back of his mind.

Not just any others, but those of his kind who were unmated.

Humans seemed invulnerable to the unnatural insanity his arousal caused, and so were shifters, or at least he'd thought so. Was that why the man had chased after him? Quinn shook his head. Most likely the shifter had guessed he was a trancer because he'd taken off at a dead run in the other direction. The action was as guilt-revealing as a criminal bolting the moment he saw a human police officer. Quinn might as well have raised a red flag and announced he was a trancer intruding upon enemy territory.

With an exasperated huff, he berated himself for being so foolish while shading in the forms of the other two males. One had been nearly as tall as the stranger, with flowing, tawny hair that had reached past his shoulders, and a frame that had appeared just as imposing. The other had been shorter but the mass of his body more than made up for what he lacked in height. Quinn knew the animal spirit each shifter was born with often resembled the person, and if the shorter man's size was anything to go on, his spirit must be a bull or an ox. His closely cropped, brown hair and goatee seemed to accentuate his wide features and stern face.

As he sketched in the details of the surroundings, Quinn's gaze strayed to the folded piece of paper on his nightstand. Typed on it was the acceptance to an application he'd put in over three weeks ago. The job wasn't glamorous, but the location was out in the middle of nowhere surrounded by miles of uninhabited forest. The promise of solitude, as well as the abundance of nature, called to him more than anything else had in his life.

With his bachelor's degree in accounting, he was capable of getting much better jobs, but those would require him to live in densely populated areas such as the one in which he currently resided. There would be no opportunity to hide from the general public as he'd been able to do by taking most of his classes online, and the strain of keeping his libido in check would only get worse.

Chapter Two

Quinn stiffened as his sensitive hearing picked up the turn of a key in the front door.

"Quinny? Quinn, where are you?"

Stifling a curse at the sound of Mara's voice, he hurriedly closed his sketchbook and hid it under a pillow. He'd completely forgotten about abandoning Cassie at the café. They'd planned to go on to lunch for a pre-celebration of his graduation, but that hadn't happened owing to unforeseen circumstances. He couldn't blame Cassie for contacting his sister. Both worried about him more than his own mother ever had, and protected him more fiercely than a mother bear did her cubs.

Mara burst into his room with Cassie and Shannon close on her heels. Dark wisps that had pulled free from her long, black braid clung to her sweat-slicked forehead as though she'd been running a marathon. Cassie's blonde curls were wind-blown, her light blue eyes wide with fright in her pixie face. Even Shannon, Mara's appointed guardian, who had the build of a professional athlete and the skills of a trained killer, appeared to be just as upset as her companions.

"Are you okay? What happened?" Mara ran to the bed, moving her hands fervently as she checked his body for injuries.

Quinn felt his cheeks heat and batted her hands away. "Nothing. I'm fine."

Cassie jumped onto the bed on his other side and slapped a hand to her chest. "Jeez, you scared the skittles out of me! I got my coffee and the next thing I knew, you were gone. Why didn't you wait for me?"

"Sorry. I wasn't feeling good."

All three women slanted their eyes shrewdly and Cassie shook her head, calling his bluff. "You were practically bouncing with excitement at the café. Was it another panic attack? Was someone rude to you?"

"No, I..." Quinn huffed as he realized they weren't going to back down until he gave them something. He loved all of them, but sometimes their over-protectiveness could be more annoying than helpful. "I lost control. There was a guy —"

Cassie gasped as a hand flew to her mouth. "Did we interrupt something? Were you...?"

"No!" If his face grew any hotter, it would burst into flames. He hadn't jerked off since he was a teenager, but even if he did, that was the last thing he'd want to discuss with his sister and her girlfriend. Shannon, he knew, would never ask him about his private life, but neither would she stop Mara and Cassie from doing so.

Mara's dove-gray eyes shone with sorrowful compassion as she tucked a lock of his hair behind one ear. "You felt attraction toward another man." When Quinn nodded, she pulled him into a tight hug. "Honey, it's okay to get turned on. Not every man is out to hurt you. One day you'll realize that arousal is nothing to fear or be ashamed of."

Quinn shuddered at her innocent words. She didn't know. She hadn't been there when his arousal had set off a riot among a crowd of his own kind that had nearly caused his death. All she knew of was the pain and humiliation he'd been forced to endure afterward and, as far as he was concerned, that was all she needed to know.

She squeezed him tighter then kissed his forehead before drawing back. "How are you feeling?"

"I'm okay." When Mara frowned, he offered a smile to cover the turbulent emotions churning in his gut. "Really, I'm fine."

"So, he must've been quite a hunk, huh?" Cassie piped up.

Quinn rolled his eyes. "Cassie."

"Oh, come on! He must have been gorgeous to make you lose control. Did he have bulging biceps? Did you check out his package?"

"Cassie!"

The woman tipped her head back and cackled loudly, then tugged him into a crushing embrace. "I'm sorry, I can't help it. You're so cute when you get flustered. I just wanna hug you and love you and squeeze you all over!"

Kill me. Now. Some days, it just didn't pay to get up in the morning, and this was definitely one of them. "I got a job offer," he blurted, needing to change the subject quickly.

Cassie pulled away and blinked at him.

"From the guy?" Mara asked.

"No. I applied for a position as an accountant and I think I want to take it. The job is in Idaho." The pained expression on his sister's beautiful face tore at his insides and he silently cursed his thoughtlessness. For all that she was his savior, he knew she'd come to rely on the comfort of his presence as much as he did hers over the past three years. Their relationship had grown immensely since she'd rescued him, despite his past trauma, or perhaps because of it. Either way, he'd known the confession of his need to strike out on his own would hurt her.

Mara swallowed convulsively then took a deep breath and smiled wanly. "I guess I knew this was coming. You're the only guy I know of to earn a BS in only two years. Someone was bound to make you an offer you couldn't resist eventually."

Quinn looked nervously at Cassie then back to Mara. "You're not mad?"

Both women frowned at him. "Why would we be mad? This is what you've studied so hard for. We're proud of you." Mara glanced at Cassie, who bobbed her head in agreement.

Quinn shrugged uncomfortably. He'd expected anger, or at the very least, resentment. The two women sitting in front of him were the very reasons for his success. None of it would have been possible without their love and guidance. After she'd rescued him, Mara had paid for his entire college tuition and Cassie had opened her heart and home to him. He owed them more than he could ever repay and, as much as he craved his independence, leaving them felt like an act of betrayal.

"Is the firm a large one?" Cassie asked. "It's probably in Boise, right? I haven't been there, but I hear it's pretty nice."

"It's actually closer to a town called Salmon, and it's not a firm. There's an older woman who runs a business out of her home helping several private business owners with their finances. She needs an assistant since her last one took a job somewhere else."

Mara's face clouded over with doubt. "Are you sure this is what you want? Idaho is so far away and it sounds like the town isn't very big. There're bound to be shifters nearby."

Quinn didn't bother to mention the employer's house was a good hour away from the town. Nor did he remind his sister that there were shifters in Sacramento as well. While their natural enemy preferred woodlands to cities, it certainly didn't mean all of them dwelled in the forests. "The woman lives with her husband and has an apartment behind her house that I can rent. I'd only be going out for groceries and supplies."

Mara opened her mouth for what he knew was probably another objection, but Cassie interrupted it by taking the woman's face in her hands and kissing the protest from her lips.

"Let him do this, sweetie. You've taught him everything he needs to know and now it's time to let him go."

Mara sighed and returned the kiss before looking back to him. "Looks like I don't have much of a choice in the matter. How will you find blood every month?"

"I'll feed from the animals there." Their blood wasn't as clean or appetizing as the blood of humans, but it was just as sustaining.

Cassie and Mara both shook their heads.

"I'll fly down there every month," Cassie said. "It's too dangerous for you to go hunting in the woods for your prey. Unless you're trying to tell me my blood isn't good enough for you anymore." She lifted one sculpted, blonde brow in challenge and he couldn't help but laugh.

"I can't ask you to do that. It's too expensive."

"I'm not asking. I'm telling you this is what's going to happen. Mara and I have long ago discussed this possibility and we're not giving you a choice in the matter. Are we, babe?"

Mara smiled adoringly at her human girlfriend and shook her head again.

For the thousandth time, Quinn wondered why his sister didn't just claim the woman who'd captured her heart like no one but a true mate could. It was so obvious what they were to each other, regardless of their kind's rigid beliefs. Not only were same-sex relationships frowned upon, but all trancers were told they could only mate with those of their own race. However, not everything the elders told them was true. The creature inside him was living testimony to that fact and marked him as different from his kind, but he refused to believe the entity was unnatural, as his father had so brutally tried to beat into him.

"No, we're not." To Quinn, Mara asked, "When are you planning to leave?"

Quinn grimaced. "I was supposed to leave yesterday. I know I should've told you sooner, but I wasn't sure of whether I wanted to go or not until now." He'd almost convinced himself to stay for his sister's sake, but his disturbing reaction to the stranger had made up his mind. The sooner he isolated himself from potential disasters like that, the better.

"Oh. Well, I guess you'd better get packed then. We're still going out tonight to celebrate your graduation, though, so you can't leave any earlier than tomorrow. I want names, addresses, phone numbers and travel times."

Quinn smirked and nodded.

"And you'd better take your car into the shop now to make sure it'll make the trip."

He nodded again.

"And no stopping for hitchhikers. You end up in a body bag and I'll have to reanimate your corpse so I can kill you for your stupidity."

"Mara!" Cassie gasped.

"Like you wouldn't do the same."

Her girlfriend giggled her agreement then jumped off the bed. "Come on, sweetie. Let's give him time to get ready."

Mara kissed him on the lips briefly then followed Cassie out of the room. Quinn was about to get up to call his new employer when he noticed Shannon still standing just inside the doorway to his room. The tall woman caught his gaze and held it with her stern, light-brown eyes.

"I can't go with you. I am the *meraan's* protector."

Quinn acknowledged her statement with a nod, hearing what he knew she wouldn't say aloud. Shannon was warning him that, should he leave, she would no longer be able to protect him as she did his sister. Two decades ago, Shannon had sworn an oath to her king, Quinn's father, to guard Mara's life with her own, but when Mara had taken Quinn in, Shannon had been forced to choose her allegiance. By aiding and abetting her princess in keeping Quinn's presence a secret, she had essentially gone against her king and accepted the risk of a death sentence should her actions be discovered.

Shannon had hated him at first, as much for forcing her to choose between her *meraan* and her king, as for the potential punishment Mara would suffer if the king found out they were harboring his fugitive son. Yet, somehow, over the years, she'd grown to be as protective over him as Mara and Cassie. The appreciation he felt for her sacrifice on his and his sister's behalves swelled in his chest and he smiled gratefully.

"Thank you."

Shannon tilted her head and took one hesitant step forward. "I could find your brother."

"No," he said a little too quickly. "I mean, I'll be okay on my own. I want to do this." And wanted to stay the hell away from anyone he'd known in his past. It wasn't that he hated Rowan. His brother had always been there for him before... Quinn gave himself a mental shake. Rowan was loved by their parents and next in line to become king. There was no need to screw up his life and beliefs by revealing the hidden embarrassment of the family Quinn had become. But, more than that, Quinn knew he couldn't handle it if his brother rejected him.

Better to live as a shadow than to set oneself up for more pain.

Shannon pursed her lips and Quinn had to look away, hoping she would let it go. Like Mara, she thought Rowan would rejoice at being reunited with his little brother after so many years, but they'd left the decision up to Quinn, just as Shannon did now. The warrior dipped her head and silently left the room.

* * * *

By seven the next morning, Quinn's belongings were packed in his VW Jetta and he was bombarded with kisses and dozens of last-minute, farewell hugs before he was finally able to hit the road. Merebeth, his new employer, had assured him the job was still available and had given him directions on how to get to her house. Fifteen hours later, long after the sun had set, he found himself standing outside of a quaint, two-story cottage with a smaller building behind it and a large garage to the side.

Unbridled joy swept through him as the enormity of his accomplishment hit home.

He was living his own destiny and embarking down a path that had once been denied him. The reality of his venture seemed almost too great to believe. His creature rumbled its delight at the thrill of being surrounded by so much uninhibited nature and he chuckled. *Are you talking to me again?* Quinn felt it sniff indignantly but continue to hum happily. The entity had remained quiet ever since he'd admonished it for wanting to stay with the stranger, and Quinn had missed their internal communication.

All the lights were on inside the cottage and he knocked on the white-painted door then took a few steps back. A minute passed and he smiled as the door opened to reveal a slightly plump woman. And the distinct scent of a shifter.

Quinn froze in shock. His sister's warning came back to him as a sick feeling settled in the pit of his stomach. He'd taken every precaution, been prepared for every possible scenario, except for this one. He didn't know how long he'd stood there gaping, but was suddenly shaken from his stupor when the woman stepped through the doorway and moved closer.

Her face held a timeless youth in her soft features, but a wealth of wisdom shone in her wide, amber eyes. Long hair in shades of gold, brown and light blonde was swept up in a loose bun with curling strands falling across her pink cheeks. She was only about an inch taller than him, but something about her countenance made her seem larger than life. Quinn took an involuntary step back but stopped when she placed a staying hand on his arm.

"You're him. Sweet Mother," she murmured in amazement. "I thought... But I wasn't sure. I didn't want to get my hopes up. You look so good!"

Before he could blink, the woman threw herself at him, enveloping him in a surprisingly strong hug. She laughed brightly then tucked her face into the crook of his neck and inhaled deeply. *Did she just sniff me?* His alarm was increasing by the second. Satisfaction glowed in her face as she pulled back to appraise him. Then, faster than he could react, she tugged him into the cottage and closed the door behind them.

"George! Come and see who it is."

Quinn's panic rose as he tried to extract his arm without success. If he bolted too quickly, she might become suspicious and discover he was a trancer, but staying was out of the question. Her bizarre greeting alone was enough reason to get out of there as soon as possible. This would have been his first job, but he was fairly certain no employer welcomed their new hire with this much enthusiasm.

"Merebeth, I'm sorry, but an emergency came up—"

"Nonsense. You're safe here and I don't bite. Much." When his steps faltered as she pulled him through a well-furnished living room and into a large, fully stocked kitchen, she tipped her head back and laughed loudly. "I'm just kidding. The only one I bite around here is George." She leaned in and whispered conspiratorially, "And he likes it!"

Quinn could only stare in utter confusion as she released his arm and pushed him onto a barstool next to an island in the middle of the kitchen.

"Wait, is that a French accent I hear?"

"Umm... Yeah. I was born in France." He cringed inwardly at the thoughtless admission. Nearly all trancers originated from France as it was their homeland and where most of them chose to stay under the protection of their king.

Merebeth only patted his arm soothingly. "It's okay, dear. I know you're *Vam'kir*. Try to calm down. You're scaring your spirit and I can feel his fear. George!"

Quinn sat in stunned silence as the woman took several items from the refrigerator and placed them on the counter. How could she know about the creature that lived inside him? Only two people in the world knew about it, not including him, and they hadn't been nearly as accepting of it as she seemed to be.

"You must be starving after that long trip. I don't have any blood, but I do have some rare roast beef." Merebeth chuckled heartily then shook her head. "Listen to me. You only drink blood on the full moon. I should've remembered that. Will a sandwich do? I'll make two. You're so much smaller than I thought you would be, but it's probably because you haven't shifted yet. Ah well, that will change soon. Would you prefer soda or water?"

Quinn was about to get up to make another attempt at escape when a tall man came in, wiping grease from his hands on an orange rag. He had a thick mane of red hair and the build of a hard laborer, but his face was creased with laugh lines and his eyes held the same kindness that glowed in Merebeth's. Quinn gained the distinct impression that they were mates and was proven correct when the man walked over to Merebeth and kissed her lovingly on the cheek.

"Will you take a look at my car tomorrow?" she asked him. "I think the brakes are going out."

"Start braking sooner," the man said gruffly. Merebeth scowled at him but he'd already turned to face Quinn. "So this is him, huh? Are you sure?"

Merebeth beamed and nodded excitedly. George tossed the rag onto the island then walked around it to offer his hand. Quinn stood abruptly and backed away. He could sense there was no aggression in the man, but he was still Quinn's enemy. With one phone call, they could have him exported from the country and into the hands of his father, or worse.

The smile on the lips of both shifters slowly faded, and George lowered his hand as he took a long step back.

"We won't hurt you," Merebeth said softly. "This is your home now for as long as you need it."

Quinn shook his head in an effort to clear his confusion. "I came here for a job."

"And you found a family. It may be some time before you're ready to meet the rest of the community, but we'll cross that road when we come to it."

He stiffened as realization flooded in. The houses and buildings he'd passed on his way to Merebeth's cottage that hadn't been a part of Salmon or on the map hadn't simply been a small, unmarked town. That had been a shifter community. He'd unwittingly traveled right into enemy territory. Merebeth's home was located on the outskirts, but that was still far too close for comfort.

"He was raised by trancers," George said with a hard edge to his tone.

Merebeth sighed and took a seat on a stool across the island from Quinn. "Our kind has been no better than the trancers in the past. Your people... They didn't tell you who you really are, did they? No, of course not. If they had, you wouldn't be here right now. Well, that doesn't matter. You're here now and it's my job to help you learn."

"Learn what?" Quinn asked hesitantly.

She smiled then got up and left the kitchen. Moments later, she returned to place a thick, leather-bound book on the counter beside him. "If I told you, I would be influencing you and this is something you need to come to terms with on your own. Your job is secure if you still want it and you can work out of the apartment around back. Since you're unmated, I'll restrict all visitors to my house and George will make sure that you have privacy, though whether you choose to stay or not, this book is yours. It will explain everything you need to know."

She fixed Quinn with an intent stare then said, "*Miel se Luuda* brought you here for a reason, Quinn. Trust in her and listen to your spirit. They will always guide you."

Quinn glanced from the book to Merebeth then back again, pretty sure the Mother of Creation wasn't responsible for his current situation. This had to be the most bizarre conversation he'd ever had in his life. None of it made sense, and all of it screamed at him to run in the other direction, yet he found that he couldn't. The creature within him was wary, but it emitted the same reluctance to leave as it had in the case of the stranger. The emotion wasn't nearly as powerful, but it was there, and this time Quinn didn't have the strength or desire to fight it.

The hunger for answers was too great to resist. In less than five minutes, the woman in front of him had voiced a better understanding of him than anyone who'd known him throughout his entire life.

He could let his fear control him, and run back to his sister, leaving the craziness of this night behind.

Looking at the eager yet patient expressions of Merebeth and her mate, he knew they wouldn't stop him. Unlike most of his kind, he'd never believed shifters were inherently evil, just as he knew trancers weren't, even though certain members of his own race had hurt him more than his enemy ever could.

"Can I think about this? It's a little…"

"Overwhelming?" Merebeth supplied. "I suppose George's approach could do with a bit more subtlety."

A slow grin lifted Quinn's lips as the other man grunted and rolled his eyes. The woman leaned in close and whispered, "I'll work on him," then in a louder voice said, "Now about those sandwiches. George will help you carry your things to the apartment."

Merebeth went back to the counter and started piling lunchmeats onto slices of bread while George motioned for Quinn to follow him to the front door. Outside, the older man hefted two suitcases from the Jetta's trunk as Quinn grabbed his backpack and a duffel bag from the backseat.

"You'll have to excuse her," George said. "She's waited a long time to meet you."

Quinn paused, not sure what to make of that. "Who are you?"

George unlocked the door to the apartment at the back of the cottage and waved him inside. "She is the historian, and I am the keeper of the sanity."

Quinn frowned at the man's cryptic words, but George didn't elaborate. After a quick tour of the furnished one-bedroom rental, George gave him the key then left. Merebeth bustled in a few minutes later with two sandwiches and the book she'd shown him earlier. Back at the entrance, she hesitated and glanced over at him. Her mouth opened and Quinn could see the urge to say something written on her face, but she merely waved him goodnight and walked out.

Quinn left the food on the coffee table, took the book to the bedroom and laid it beside him as he sat on the bed. In italicized, old English lettering on the cover was written *Ba'Kal*, the formal name for shifters, and underneath that was written *Vam'kir*, the formal name for trancers. Long into the night, he stared at the cover, unable to look away but afraid to lift it. When the sun finally peeked over the horizon and shone through the window, illuminating the small room, he let out a sigh and set about unpacking his belongings. Once finished, he returned to the bed, sat against the headboard with the book in his lap and began to read.

Chapter Three

Manning gripped the steering wheel and resisted the urge to bash his head against it. He was beginning to think Tailor was right in suggesting his strong reaction to the shifter he'd seen in Sacramento had merely been a product of stress as well as the combination of an overworked desire to find his mate and an alluring scent. Problem was, his mind wouldn't let it go. The image of the man he'd been hunting for the past two weeks popped into his thoughts every time he closed his eyes. The aromas of chocolate and rain triggered his memory and drove him harder.

He'd searched every inch of Sacramento and come up with nothing. No one in the community near the city had ever seen a shifter fitting the man's description, and there was no other community in the state of California. Cain had convinced him to return to his hometown to catch up with the investigation's affairs, but once that was done, he planned on revisiting Sacramento to expand his search.

Manning put his car in gear and headed for his hometown from the airport. He would have to see his father and relate the news of his mate's discovery and subsequent failure to keep him, but he needed answers first. As far as he knew, there had never been a same-sex mating in his ancestral line. Each generation of his house was born to rule over all the communities, therefore it was necessary to produce heirs. How was he supposed to do that with a male mate?

While he saw nothing wrong with gay men, or women, it'd never occurred to him that he might end up with a male partner for a mate. Funny, however, that when he'd seen the shifter outside the café, what was between his legs hadn't mattered. Nor had he considered the dilemma of carrying on his line. All he'd been able to think about was marking him, claiming him and never letting him go. It had been an almost mindless compulsion and one that was more than a little disconcerting. The man had been scared and Manning honestly couldn't say whether he would be able to control himself if he saw the stranger again.

Manning shook that thought from his head. He would never harm his mate, and when he found him again, he would do whatever it took to convince him to stay.

At the end of a long dirt road, he pulled up in front of the historian's cottage and got out. He probably should've called first but knew she wouldn't mind him dropping in. Merebeth and his mother had been close friends since they were little girls and had shared in his upbringing since Merebeth had never been able to have children of her own.

Manning knocked on the front door then took a look around the yard while he waited. With a grin, he noticed that George was still tinkering with his old, beat-up Chevy truck on the side of the house. He turned back as the door opened and was greeted with a huge smile.

"Manning! It's so good to see you. How's your father?" She came out and hugged him tightly.

"I just got back and haven't seen him yet, but he said he was fine over the phone. How have you been?"

"Wonderful. I've got a new assistant and he's a genius with the numbers. Have you had any luck with finding your mate?"

Manning shifted uncomfortably and scrubbed a hand through his hair. "That's what I came here to talk to you about. Can we go inside?"

"No."

He paused with one hand on the doorknob, not sure he'd heard the woman correctly. "No?"

"No. It's such a beautiful day, we can talk out here." She took his hand and led him to the porch swing where she pushed him down and sat next to him. "Go ahead. I'm all ears."

With a frown, he glanced at the door then back to Merebeth. "Is everything all right?" As her *Jaes'din,* he had the right to demand entrance, though he would never abuse his power like that. Merebeth had always kept an open door policy. As the historian of their race, she went out of her way to make everyone feel welcome and encouraged them to study their heritage.

Merebeth crinkled her eyes and bit her bottom lip. "My assistant is a little shy around company. It may take him a while to open up, but that's neither here nor there. What's on your mind?"

After a deep breath, he said, "I found my mate, but he's a man."

Merebeth's blonde brows shot up. "And that bothers you?"

"I don't know. I've never been attracted to men, but I can't deny that he's my mate. Have you ever heard of a *Jaes'din* having a male mate?"

"Ah," she said, patting his hand. "You're worried about having offspring. I don't think there's ever been a male descendent of your line that has mated with another male, but that's not to say it can't happen, or that it's a bad thing. These days, there are so many ways to have children that I don't think it'll be a problem."

Manning sat back and mulled over that for a few minutes. The issue of carrying on his line he could put to rest. "I found my mate while I was out visiting the community in California, but—" His words were cut off as the front door opened and a man carrying a large book came out. Shoulder-length black hair hid his face as he traced a line in the book with one finger.

"Merebeth, what does *Ju'kul te armend* mean?"

Arousal slammed into Manning as the vision, the scent of the shifter, overwhelmed his senses. It was his mate, the man who had possessed his dreams and every waking moment for the past two weeks. Manning's heartbeat kicked into overdrive and he fought to keep his canines from dropping as he stood and faced the other man. His mate looked up sharply with a mixture of confusion and surprise on his face.

Up close, he was more stunning than Manning remembered. His pale skin shone in the afternoon sun and his soft features were off-set by black lashes and full, dark lips. Manning was once again struck by how small he was compared to other shifters. His body was slender yet defined under the cover of a snug T-shirt and jeans. Light gray eyes sparkled as they met and held Manning's gaze.

Then, just as before, he took off.

Manning sprinted after him through the front door and living room. Merebeth shouted for him to stop, but he ignored her. This was his mate and no one had a right to keep the man from him. In the kitchen, he skidded to a halt as the man ran to the other side and put his back to the wall, panting with the book clutched tightly to his chest. There was no other way out except through him and Manning had no intention of stepping aside until he got some answers.

"Whoa, what's going on here?" George moved from the sink to place his body between Manning and the other man, and Merebeth quickly did the same, as though protecting his mate.

What the hell *was* going on here? Did they honestly think he would harm the smaller man?

"He's my mate. I just want to talk to him," Manning answered with hands raised in a calming manner.

Merebeth sucked in a breath and looked back at the man. "Quinn, is this true?"

Quinn's eyes were wild as he shook his head. Manning could smell the faint scent of lust from the man, his mate's body naturally responding to his, but it was nearly drowned out by the stench of fear.

"Manning, George, why don't you two give me and Quinn some time to talk?"

George nodded to his mate then started toward Manning. "Come on. I've got a beauty of a cracked cylinder head we can take a look at."

Manning growled and refused to budge when the older man took his arm. "He ran from me in Sacramento. I want to know what's going on before I let him out of my sight again."

Merebeth whipped around and placed both hands on her hips. "Manning Joseph Stone, don't think you're too old for me to teach you a lesson in manners. If he is your mate, you need to show some respect and give him time to make his own decision."

Manning winced at the reprimand, knowing she was right. He'd never been a brute, and starting with his mate wasn't going to get him answers any sooner. But getting his body to retreat was like trying to move a wall of granite. His feline was less than pleased and not slacking in its effort to let him know.

To Quinn, he said, "I'll be outside when you're ready to talk."

But his mate wouldn't look at him or acknowledge his words. Painfully, he turned and followed George out of the cottage and around to the dilapidated truck at the side of the yard. The other man didn't even try to distract him with auto talk or anything else Manning wouldn't have been able to concentrate on. He simply sat on the wooden bench next to the Chevy and gestured for Manning to join him.

"He isn't like other shifters," George commented after a prolonged silence.

Manning snorted but held his tongue. He'd gathered that within ten seconds of first sighting the man. The spirits that lived within all shifters were predatory by nature, and while his race was as capable of feeling fear as any other, they typically didn't choose flight over fight.

"He wasn't raised by us, Manning. He's...a rare individual, and I think whoever had him before took advantage of that."

Manning narrowed his gaze, but it went unnoticed as George eyed his truck as though he could fix it if he stared hard enough. "What are you saying, that he was raised by humans?" It would explain why no one in the Sacramento community knew of him.

"I'm saying you need to keep an open mind. You screw this up and you're not the only one who will suffer. The future of our race depends on how you treat that boy. I've known you since you were a cub and patience ain't one of your strong points, but that's exactly what he needs."

A surge of anger swept through Manning at the affront to his pride. "I would never hurt him, and I've already talked to Merebeth about finding a way to carry on my line. If Quinn wants to have a child, I have no problem with that, but most likely it'll be mine that takes over after me as the *Jaes'din*."

George sent him an incredulous look then laughed. "Well, it's good to know you've got all your puppies in a row, but that's not what I meant. Quinn is...special. What he can bring to our race is more important than anything you could accomplish in a lifetime, and that's including giving us heirs. No offense, son."

As he reined in his frustration over the vague words, Manning ground out, "Are you going to tell me what the hell it is you're trying to say or keep me guessing?"

George released an aggrieved sigh. "No patience. It's his story to tell, but I will say this. It's taken my mate two weeks to crack that boy's shell. You ruin all of her hard work and you'll pay. Man, will you pay."

Great. He felt much better. His questions had increased tenfold and his life was in potential danger from a woman half his size. "Is there anything else I need to know?"

"Nope. Think that about sums it up from me."

Manning grunted and lapsed into silence. His irritation was only held in check by the knowledge that his mate was near and that this time there would be no running. If he had to, he'd camp out on Merebeth's porch to keep the man from getting away. They sat together for the better part of an hour. When the front door finally opened again and Quinn came out, Manning stood to face him. George mumbled something about a leak needing to be fixed then left them alone.

His mate stopped several yards away. He reminded Manning of a skittish colt as he stood there shifting from foot to foot. Manning scrambled for something to say to break the tension and ultimately decided humility was best. "I'm sorry if I scared you."

Quinn frowned and met his gaze directly. "I'm not afraid of you. I don't even know you."

It was Manning's turn to frown. "Then why did you run from me?"

Quinn shrugged one shoulder and looked away.

"George told me you weren't raised by our kind. Do you know what a mate is?" Manning asked.

"Yes, and I don't want one. You can find yourself another guy to mate with."

"Actually, I was never into guys." Manning cursed himself the moment the words left his mouth.

Quinn gaped then pivoted on his heel, striding back to the door.

"Wait! I'm sorry. I didn't mean for it to come out like that." He'd almost caught up to Quinn when his mate spun around and pinned him with a furious glare. A grin played at the corners of his mouth and it took all that he had not to let it break free. The man was breathtaking in his anger, with gray eyes that darkened and high color staining his cheeks.

"Then find a female! I don't care. I will never bond with you."

Interesting. The subtle hint of Quinn's French accent became more pronounced with the rise of his emotions. The accentuated lilt was provocative in an innocent way that went straight to Manning's cock. With no small amount of effort, he tamped down his desire and kept his expression neutral.

"Then at least give me a chance to get to know you. Let me take you out on a date."

"If it weren't for my scent, you wouldn't want to have anything to do with me."

Manning shook his head. "I noticed you before I ever smelled you." And it was true. Quinn had caught his eye before Manning had ever taken in the other man's scent. He remembered everything about that first moment. "You were wearing a long-sleeved, blue-striped shirt about two sizes too big for you and jeans that required a belt to keep them up. You had on white tennis shoes and carried a coffee cup that you dropped when you ran. Your hair was hiding most of your face, but I still remember the way your gray eyes glittered in the light, like they're doing now. I would have noticed you anywhere."

Quinn stared at him for several excruciating minutes. Manning wanted to add more but was afraid of overdoing it. Fear, he could deal with, but his mate was outright refusing their bond and that put him on a whole new playing field. He had no idea how to woo a man, but he had a feeling he was going to learn, and quickly. Another grin tried to escape as he watched Quinn gnaw on his bottom lip.

"I don't like going out."

Manning's heart rate spiked with excitement. Quinn's comment wasn't a 'no'. "We can stay in. I can make you dinner. Have you tasted Merebeth's cooking yet?"

"Of course. I live right behind her."

Quinn was her new assistant. He didn't know why he hadn't made the connection sooner. Some of his tension eased at that fact. If his mate tried to leave, he would have to take the time to pack all his things, and that would give Manning plenty of time to change the man's mind.

If it ever came to that. Which it wouldn't.

"Well, she taught me, so I'm not half bad."

His mate glanced at the cottage with a reluctant expression. "Would it be at your place?"

From the tone of Quinn's voice, Manning guessed that wasn't a preferable option. "We can eat here if you want. I'm sure Merebeth and George wouldn't mind."

"Not at all!" Merebeth yelled as she popped her head out of the living room window. Quinn's face grew bright red and the grin Manning had been fighting finally broke through. "We were just thinking about how nice it would be to go into town for dinner. You two can have the whole house to yourselves. That apartment is way too small."

"No. You don't have to—" Quinn protested.

"I'll see you at seven, then," Manning said as he walked swiftly to his car. Once behind the wheel, he waved and pulled out of the driveway, confident that Merebeth would work her magic on Quinn. As he headed home to meet with his father, his thoughts strayed to the way Merebeth and George had shown their willingness to protect his mate. After only a short time, it seemed Quinn had worked his way into the couple's hearts, which was odd considering the fact that he didn't belong to a community and was apparently from a country predominantly occupied by trancers. Their affection for him, however, was unmistakable. Manning had to admit that there was something about Quinn that was unusual and compelling, yet at the same time, familiar.

Whatever it was, he couldn't wait to explore it further.

* * * *

Temptation stared blatantly at him in the form of a set of keys hanging on the wall in the kitchen. He could still leave. Merebeth and George were gone for the evening and Manning wasn't supposed to arrive for another thirty minutes. He could drive around for an hour then come back to enjoy the rest of the night alone.

And admit his cowardice to Merebeth in the morning.

Quinn sighed and rubbed at his eyes. He couldn't do that to the woman who had given him so much. Because of her, he'd been able to come to terms with what he was and the creature inside him. *Not creature. Spirit.* The book Merebeth had given him was full of answers he'd been searching for his entire life. He was only a quarter of the way through it so far. Everything was written in either the *Ba'Kal* language or his native *Vam'kir* tongue. They were strikingly similar, which allowed him to learn the *Ba'Kal* language quickly, but it was still going to take some time.

It described the traits, traditions and customs of both races, which were also remarkably alike. Both had ruling houses that governed over all of their respective communities. They worshiped the same divine creator, *Miel se Luuda*, and lived their lives by the cycles of the moon. The only major differences were that *Ba'Kal* were born with the spirit of an animal that they could take the form of at any time, with the exception of the nights during the full moon when the change was involuntary. *Vam'kir,* on the other hand, ingested the blood of humans, but that was also only necessary during the full moon.

In the old days, the *Vam'kir* had used their ability to put their victims into a trance in order to keep their existence a secret, hence their nickname, but that had changed roughly a century ago when Quinn's grandfather had allowed the *Vam'kir* to choose select humans to become donors for their kind.

The book had gone in depth on the relationship between a shifter and its spirit, and Quinn had been unable to deny it was the same relationship he shared with the entity within him. The concept of being born with the characteristics of both races was one that he was still learning to deal with. As far as he knew, there were no others like him. Even if it were possible for *Ba'Kal* and *Vam'kir* to procreate together, his mother couldn't have had an affair with a shifter at the time of his conception, for it had occurred during a small war and she'd been restricted to the fortress for months.

Merebeth had promised him he would find the answers to the rest of his questions in the book, and he trusted her. How could he not, when learning that his spirit was a natural gift and not a curse as his father had tried to convince him? He'd never blindly hated shifters with the passion of the majority of his people, and the discovery that he was one of them was surprisingly easy to accept.

That didn't mean he wanted to mate with one, however. His past contained too much shit and he couldn't chance that his arousal would have the same effect on unmated shifters as it did on unmated trancers. No matter how great Merebeth claimed this Manning to be, Quinn couldn't subject the man to a life of necessary seclusion, and that's what it would be if they bonded.

Quinn started at the sound of a knock and, taking a deep breath to steady his nerves, rose from the couch and went to the door. He could handle this. All he had to do was control his libido long enough for the man to lose interest. Mates were so rare, most trancers and shifters went their entire lives without finding theirs. Instead, they learned to love others with whom they were compatible. Manning would give up eventually, and Quinn would go on with his life.

As he opened the door, the strong scents of pine and musk flowed into his lungs and heated his blood. Manning's large frame filled the doorway, covered in a white, button-down shirt and black jeans that hugged his lean hips and long legs. He held several grocery bags in one hand and a bottle of wine in the other. Desire hit Quinn hot and hard as he tipped his head back to look up at the man's handsome face. He immediately quelled his arousal and searched for signs of mindless lust in the dark gaze that met his, but there was only a hint of amusement.

Manning quirked one corner of his mouth up in a crooked grin and asked, "Can I come in?"

"Sorry." Quinn moved aside to let him pass then closed the door. He eyed the man warily, following him to the kitchen and watched him pull several items from the bags and set them by the stove.

"Merebeth told me you like red meat, which is good because I've got about ten pounds of steak in my freezer. I'm a bit of a meat eater myself," Manning said with a smile, revealing a dimple on his right cheek. "She also said you weren't a fan of vegetables, but I figured potatoes were a safe bet. Go ahead and take a seat at the table. I know my way around the kitchen."

Quinn scowled as he walked over to the table and sat on one of the chairs. Apparently, both Merebeth and his spirit were set on conspiring against him. "What else did she tell you?"

"That if I burned her kitchen down, she'd make me build her a new one."

With a soft laugh, he traced the lines in the rough, wood surface of the table in an attempt to abate his nervousness. When he noticed Manning had stopped moving to stare at him, he looked up again. "What?"

"You're beautiful when you smile."

Despite his effort to remain detached, warmth flushed through him and he squirmed in the chair.

"So what did Merebeth say to convince you to come out and talk to me?" Manning asked.

"She said I would have to meet with you to be accepted into the community." He didn't particularly care to be, but apparently, since he was a shifter, it was a requirement. All he cared about was doing his job and staying with the only two people who knew what he was and had befriended him regardless.

"Actually, the decision is up to the community's Alpha, but I'll put in a good word."

"I thought you were the leader here?"

Manning hesitated as he put the potatoes in the oven. "We don't exactly have leaders. Each Alpha is in charge of his community and regulates our laws much as a human sheriff does. I oversee the actions of the Alphas and modify the laws according to what's necessary for the safety of each community."

A wave of nausea rolled through Quinn's stomach as he recalled a section of the book he'd read. "You're the *Jaes'din*."

Manning studied his reaction then nodded. "Does that intimidate you?"

Yes. No. Because there would be no bonding between them. Quinn didn't think Merebeth would have eagerly pushed him into this meeting if Manning were the type to try to force him into bonding like his father had tried to do, or at least he hoped not. "Of course not."

The other man chuckled, letting Quinn know his lie hadn't fooled either of them. "Just as long as you're sure. Let's go sit in the living room while the food cooks." He filled two wine glasses and handed one to Quinn.

In the next room, they sat on either ends of the couch facing each other. The conversation was kept light and Quinn found himself relaxing under the man's easy-going manner. He tried to keep his answers monosyllabic, but that didn't deter Manning's interest in him. The only time the man slipped was at the point when Quinn started talking about his job and Manning developed that blank, smile-and-nod reflex so many people did when he went into the details of his work. He laughed at the man's expression and Manning grinned sheepishly, admitting he'd never been good at numbers.

Quinn discovered they had a lot more in common than he would've guessed. Both preferred reading to watching TV and wine to beer. They also both hated shopping and had studied mythology in college. Manning appeared extremely impressed by the fact that Quinn had earned his bachelor's degree in just over two years and couldn't seem to stop complimenting him over it. When the buzzer sounded on the oven, the large man got up to fix their plates. They ate in comfortable silence and Quinn moaned at the feel of the steak almost melting on his tongue.

Manning groaned immediately afterward, saying, "You shouldn't make noises like that."

Quinn swallowed then opened his mouth to ask why but felt his breath catch at the half-lidded look of stark arousal in the other man's eyes. He quickly glanced away, biting hard on the inside of his cheek to hold back his answering flare of lust.

"How old are you, Quinn?"

He sighed in relief at the change of subject. "Twenty-five."

"Have you ever had a girlfriend or...boyfriend?"

"Yeah, a boyfriend, when I was a teenager."

Manning took a bite of his potato then asked, "Were you in love with him?"

Quinn smiled at the memory of Sean. They'd been best friends since childhood, and eventually that friendship had blossomed into love. Sean had been everything to him. They'd even fancied themselves mates and had decided to wait until the perfect time, after high school and before college, to exchange blood and prove their bond to their families, and that being gay and in love was not a phase they would outgrow.

"Yeah. He was nice. I thought he was my mate—"

Manning growled and put his plate on the coffee table. "I am your mate. I don't want you seeing this guy again unless I'm with you."

Quinn's body began to quake with anger at the brazen possession in the man's tone. For too long he'd been stripped of freedom by the harsh authority of others. *No more.* "I don't care who you are. You have

no right to dictate my life. I can see anyone I want to."
He stormed off to the kitchen, dumped his food in the
trash and went to the sink to wash his plate. Tears
pricked his eyes as a stabbing pain entered his chest.
The memory of Sean, of what he'd irrevocably lost,
clawed at his insides. His first love would never want
to see him again regardless. Not after what had
happened.

Chapter Four

Quinn's life had been forever altered the day of his high school graduation. He and Sean had found a hidden niche in the side of the school building while the principal was rattling off the names of their classmates and handing out diplomas. They were last on the list so they'd decided to play a little before joining the others. Sean had always been a gentle lover, and that time had been no different. Their kisses had been slow and deep, and when Sean's hand had traveled down to unbutton Quinn's pants and grip his aching member, Quinn had gasped with desire.

Then, unexpectedly, Sean's actions had become urgent. Demanding. His fangs had dropped and he'd scratched deep furrows into Quinn's skin in his rush to rip the clothes from his body. When Quinn had cried out for him to stop, Sean had merely ground his hard cock into Quinn's groin and bitten harshly into his neck. Quinn had managed to throw him off and escape, but the assault hadn't stopped there.

Every unmated male and female of age from the ceremony had chased him down and attacked him in a frenzied lust. They'd torn off his remaining clothes and bitten into every inch of his exposed body, trying to force him to submit. Only the empowered voice of his father had saved him from being viciously taken against his will right there on the school grounds. His assailants had frozen at his father's command and he'd been hauled off only to learn that his suffering had just begun.

Quinn jerked at the touch of a hand on his shoulder.

"I'm sorry. I let my jealousy get the better of me."

Manning's eyes held the glint of sincere regret, but Quinn steadfastly ignored him and went back to scouring the plate. Long fingers wrapped loosely around one of his wrists while Manning's other hand lifted to brush back the fall of his hair.

"Please don't let my stupidity ruin the rest of the night. Tell me to leave and I will, but I'd rather stay."

Quinn snapped his head up, an insult on the tip of his tongue, but the words died the moment he met the other man's pained gaze. Manning's hand cupped his cheek, his thumb sweeping across it to wipe away a tear Quinn hadn't realized had fallen. Instinctively, he leaned into the soft caress and felt his anger dissipate despite his attempt to hold onto it. For the second time that day, he succumbed to the man's persuasiveness.

They continued to stare at each other in tense silence and Quinn's gut tightened as the atmosphere slowly changed, taking on a distinct, sexually charged undercurrent. His mouth went dry as he watched Manning's eyes transform right in front of him. A faint, yellow glow lent color to the black irises, shining brighter until they burned with unbridled desire. The pupils dilated, becoming spheres that seemed to delve into Quinn's very soul. His skin tingled and blood pooled in his groin as Manning's lips inched toward his.

He should stop this. He should say something to break the spell that was dragging him under, but he couldn't. His world narrowed to the hot breath mingling with his and the enticing heat radiating from the other man. Manning paused when only centimeters separated them and it took several seconds of agonizing anticipation for Quinn to realize the man was waiting on him. Somehow, he knew nothing more would happen unless he initiated it. That knowledge alone drove away the last of his inhibitions and he leaned forward to accept the invitation.

Quinn moaned as Manning's lips met his in a soft, sensuous press. Tiny sparks played along his skin and raised the fine hairs on his neck and arms. When Manning's tongue quested across the seam of his mouth, he opened willingly, eager for a taste of the man. Spices and something else, something intoxicating, burst along his taste buds as the scents of pine and musk grew stronger. His hands moved of their own volition to Manning's back as the man's arms surrounded him, the embrace firm yet gentle.

Sensations both strange and exhilarating drowned him in their intensity. This was like nothing he'd ever experienced before, even with Sean. The kiss was deep and consuming, the strokes of Manning's tongue languid as it plundered his mouth. He was turned so that his back was pressed to the sink and the hard length of the man slid roughly against him. The arms around him increased the strength of their hold, but that only served to heighten his arousal.

Manning began swiveling his hips, rubbing their groins together until the friction he was creating had

Quinn whimpering for more. Quinn wanted this. Needed this release. So much time had passed since someone had touched him without pain or maddened lust. A few more minutes and he knew he would come. The pressure of his orgasm was building and, judging from Manning's breathless moans and increased rhythm, the man wouldn't be far behind him.

Quinn was panting now and grinding his own cock into Manning's groin. He could hear the ebb and flow of the man's blood calling to him but resisted the urge to allow his fangs to drop. Manning pulled back to whisper something in his native language and Quinn saw a flash of canines right before Manning bent down to lick his neck.

Fear snaked its way into his heart, seizing control before he knew what was happening. Memories of pain and blood coating his flesh filled his thoughts, stealing the beauty of the moment, and all he could do was react.

"No." Quinn shoved at the wall of muscle encasing him and when it didn't move, his panic spiked. "Get off of me."

Manning pulled back with a look of confusion. "Quinn?"

"Let go of me!" He pushed again and lost his balance when the large man jerked away. Manning reached out to steady him but stopped at a low snarl from Quinn.

With hands raised in a peaceful gesture, Manning took a step back. "Easy, pup. I'm not going to hurt you. Tell me what's going on."

Quinn knew he was losing touch with reality, his thoughts spiraling down a dark tunnel that didn't exist in that time. A distant part of his mind registered the truth in the words of the man in front of him, but this wasn't about Manning. This was about a past that would never let him go. The memories would forever haunt him, and he would forever be fighting a losing battle.

"Get out." Quinn clutched at the countertop, sure his knees would buckle if he let go.

"Baby, talk to me. I want to help you."

"Get away from me!" Quinn shouted. He watched in horror as Manning flinched as though physically struck, but was too far gone to regain control. He was falling apart and the last thing he wanted was for Manning to witness it. "Leave. Please leave." The words tumbled from his mouth over and over again until eventually he blinked and realized he was alone. Anger at his weakness bubbled up and he spun around, flinging one arm across the counter and sending everything on it crashing to the floor.

With the last of his failing strength, he stumbled from the house and along the short walkway to his apartment. Once inside, he headed straight for the bathroom and stripped out of his clothes. His past seemed to bleed through to reality and all he could see was the memory of blood on his body. Blood that'd coated every inch of his skin. And he shook with the need to get it off. After making the water as hot as he could stand it, he climbed into the shower and began frantically scrubbing his skin with a washcloth. He didn't know how long he'd been lost in the fog of his memories before Merebeth's shrill voice came through from the other side of the door.

"Quinn?" she shouted. "Quinn! I'm coming in. It's just me."

Only when the shower curtain was yanked to the side and he heard the woman's sharp gasp did awareness begin to seep in. He turned his body to hide his nudity, dipping his head in embarrassment and forcing his aching fingers to release the cloth before turning the water off.

"Sweet Mother of Creation, what did they do to you? My poor *Aucinthe!*" she exclaimed as he grabbed a towel from a nearby rack and wrapped it around his waist with trembling hands.

As soon as he was decently covered, she tugged him into the next room. "It's all right. You just had a little fright, is all. Lay down and I'll be right back with some tea."

Quinn sat numbly on the side of his bed while the woman hurried from the room. He could smell George's masculine scent coming from the small kitchen and hear their hushed words as Merebeth assured her mate everything was fine. She came back a minute later and sat beside him, pressing a warm mug into his hands and lifting it to his lips. The taste was rich and spread liquid fire down to his belly, the sweet liquor mixed in instantly soothing his frayed nerves.

His episodes never lasted long, and soon he slumped back against the headboard, offering Merebeth a shy smile. "I'm sorry I ruined your evening."

She shook her head adamantly. "Nonsense. You didn't ruin anything. In fact, you saved me. George had just started on another one of his tangents about his truck and I think I might have died of boredom if not for your convenient distraction."

"Why?"

Merebeth frowned. "Why what, dear?"

"Why are you doing this for me?" Confusion warred with acceptance as he tried to understand her generosity in giving him a home, answers and a friendship that went well beyond an employer-employee relationship. He knew it had something to do with the fact that he was born of both races, but he also couldn't help but feel like a burden, just as he'd been to his sister.

Merebeth sighed and gave his knee a comforting squeeze. "You are a very important person, and I can't tell you why. You have to figure it out on your own. But it's more than that. Everyone deserves a helping hand, and I'm the lucky woman here to give it to you."

Quinn nodded, knowing he wouldn't get any more out of her than that and was too grateful to argue. Much like Mara, Merebeth had a talent for calming the rage of a storm without having to know its origins or expecting anything in return. Still, there was an issue he needed to clear with her. "It wasn't him. Manning didn't do anything wrong."

"I know. He's the one who called me."

With a groan, he covered his face in further embarrassment. Merebeth merely chuckled and patted his leg.

"He's a good man. Don't give up just yet."

"He's a shifter. I'm a trancer. It's never going to work."

"You're a shifter too. And you can't tell me you don't feel anything when it comes to him. There is a reason for everything. You just have to be patient and keep your mind open. It'll work out."

Quinn shook his head but found himself grinning back at her, then felt it slip away. "I need to go back to your house. I think I might have left a mess in the kitchen."

"It's okay. I saw it on my way here. I've found that kitchenware often gets the urge to jump off countertops or from hands and commit suicide. Remember that glass I supposedly dropped last week? Suicide. Anyways, George will have it all cleaned up by morning. You just lie down and get some rest."

Merebeth got up and closed the bedroom door behind her. Quinn dressed in a pair of flannel pants and lay down but sleep eluded him. He couldn't stop replaying the scene in the kitchen with Manning, seeing images of the brilliant color fading from the man's eyes as their combined arousal had been destroyed. Quinn cursed angrily, flung the covers back and began pacing the length of his small room.

This was what he wanted. To drive the infuriating man away. If it were just about sex... Quinn laughed harshly. How ironic was that? For the first time in years, the idea of another man touching him, holding him and making his body come alive, didn't terrify him. Instead it thrilled him beyond measure. Manning was different. He'd taken charge but only after Quinn had given him permission, and not once had his actions become feral or cruel. He'd remained in control the whole time.

It was Quinn who had lost it.

But Manning wanted more than a simple night of twisted sheets and sexual release. He wanted something Quinn wasn't sure he could give—his freedom. Not after so many years of fighting to get it back. With a frustrated growl, Quinn stomped over to the window and stared out at the night sky. A glint caught his eye and he peered into the dense shadows of the trees where he saw them—two lambent, yellow orbs shining from the face of a panther blacker than the darkness surrounding it.

He knew those eyes. They had bathed him in passion and set fire to his blood only hours ago. They were soft and comforting now, unwavering as they watched him from the line of the forest. Quinn's spirit howled within him, yearning to join the animal on the other side of the window, and this time, the entity's emotions didn't feel like a betrayal. They whispered truth, but he wasn't ready yet. Quinn put his palm to the glass and watched the panther lay down on its belly, chin on its paws, as though it were settling in for the night.

When he went back to his bed, sleep came quickly, and visions of those eerie, yellow eyes dominated his dreams.

* * * *

"There have been three more attacks."

Manning paused on the steps to his porch and looked up at Cain. Tailor was there also, lounging against one of the white pillars, though his body was coiled with tension. After shifting swiftly to his human form, concentrating briefly to form clothes onto his body, Manning strode past them and into his house. "Where is my father?"

"In his room sleeping," Cain answered.

Manning nodded as he bypassed his bedroom and walked into the large bathroom next to it. He was exhausted from a night of watching over his mate and going over every detail of his first date with the man, trying to discern where he'd fucked up, but it didn't appear that rest would come anytime soon. As *Jaes'din*, he was responsible for the welfare of his race, and that took priority.

"What the hell happened to you?" Tailor asked as he hopped onto the counter and leaned back against the wide mirror behind him. "I thought you were going on a date with your mate. You look like shit."

Manning shot him an annoyed glance then stripped out of his clothes, turned on the shower and got in. "Things didn't go quite as planned. Tell me about the attacks. When did they happen?"

Cain sat down on the closed toilet lid and pinched the bridge of his nose. "One occurred last night. The home of an Alpha in Texas was vandalized. The other two happened approximately three and four weeks ago. In one case, the mate of an Alpha was murdered and in the other, it was the son of an Alpha. We believe it's the same trancers who are responsible for your mother's death because of the style, but there was a message left behind from these murders. The same two words written in blood. 'Surrender him'."

A tide of fury swept over him and he jerked aside the shower curtain. "Why wasn't I informed of this until now?"

"Apparently the Alphas wanted to deal with the matters themselves. They admitted to striking out against a few small packs of trancers but didn't find the ones who'd committed the crimes. The Alpha who was vandalized last night convinced the others to finally call you to seek out your help. None of them has a clue as to what the message means."

Manning clenched his fists to keep his claws from unsheathing as his anger mounted. He knew exactly what was going on, and even though it wasn't uncommon during a time of transition, it still infuriated him. His people were suffering the loss of their former *Jaes'din*, his father having abdicated upon the death of his mate, and were doubting Manning's ability to rule. Most likely, they saw his reluctance to take immediate revenge for his mother's murder as a sign of weakness, when in reality, that act could plunge them into a devastating war. While he realized that might be inevitable, they were still unprepared.

"Contact all of the Alphas. Let them know that any further action taken without my express permission will be punishable by banishment. If they can't follow the laws they're supposed to be enforcing, I'll have them replaced."

"And when should I tell them to meet with us here, or do you plan on holding a conference somewhere else?"

Manning finished washing off then stepped out to towel dry. He walked to his room with Tailor and Cain following and sat on the side of his bed. The hunt for the murderers would have to wait. He couldn't afford to have his attention divided as it was between revenge and securing his mate to his side. Quinn was, essentially, a flight risk, and even though they'd only known each other for one day, the thought of losing the younger man made his stomach twist nauseatingly.

"Tell them to take whatever precautions they deem necessary to ensure the safety of their communities. I'll contact them later about setting up a course of action."

"With all due respect, sir," Tailor spoke up from where he was leaning against the dresser, "I think we should take action now. All of the attacks have been aimed at the officials of our race, your house not excluded. Our enemy is obviously sending us a message that we can't ignore. That your mate is male is...unusual, but it also works in our favor. You can impregnate a willing female then take your mate with you to conduct the hunt."

Manning shook his head. "He's not ready. I need to give him more time and I don't want to move out until we're bonded."

"Your people need you to—"

"I know what my people need," Manning snapped, "but my mate needs me just as much. I will not take his choice from him simply because he's male and I have the ability to secure my line without him. We've waited this long. A few more weeks won't make the difference as long as we strengthen our defenses. Send some of our warriors to those communities who are lacking. Meanwhile, I'll set up a team of trackers to determine whether the trancers who killed my mother are the same as those who attacked the families of the Alphas."

Both men stared at him for long seconds and he stared right back. He didn't quite know why he was putting the issue of his bonding above the one that was undeniably more pressing, but he wouldn't budge on it. Tailor and Cain seemed to accept that as they both nodded simultaneously.

"We'll take care of everything while you concentrate on your mate, then," Cain said. "Let us know if we can do anything to help."

Manning thanked them then lay down after they left. His mind only allowed him a few hours' sleep, however, before it was up and running again, forcing his body into motion. Something had happened last night that had frightened Quinn, and the possibility that he might have been the cause of it was eating away at his conscience. He was sure it had been desire he'd sensed in the eyes and scent of his young mate. That Quinn had wanted his touch, his kiss.

Perhaps he'd pushed too fast, but that didn't account for the haunted look Manning had seen afterward.

Manning ground his teeth at the only other possibility he could think of. The idea that someone had hurt his mate made his vision blur with anger. Had Quinn been discovered and tortured by trancers while living in France? And what kind of parents would willingly raise their shifter child in a country where their enemy lurked around every corner?

Manning wanted answers, and he wasn't going to get them by lying in bed. Once dressed, he went to check on his father, who was having breakfast in the kitchen. Adan was still in his prime and could easily have been mistaken for Manning's brother and not a shifter ninety years his senior, but the loss of the man's mate had taken its toll. Lines creased his face and his eyes contained a hollowness that reflected the sorrow inside.

Adan looked up as Manning entered and smiled a greeting. "How did your night go?"

Manning winced and took a seat across from his father at the table. "Not exactly as I'd hoped. It's...a little complicated."

"Son, a mate is a gift, no matter what form it comes to you in."

"No, it's not that. I mean, yes, I was worried at first, but he's unlike anyone I've ever met." Quinn had an intriguing way about him that wreaked havoc on all of Manning's preconceived ideals of a mate. He was confident in some areas, yet nervous in others. He was aware of the status of a *Jaes'din's* mate, yet it meant nothing to him. And his body... Those hard, sinuous muscles that had writhed beneath Manning's hands and that steel length that had rubbed desperately against Manning's own straining cock... "No, it's definitely not that he's a man."

"Then what is it?"

"There've been three more attacks, all on the families of Alphas. I know I need to do something about it, and soon, but Quinn is..." He sighed heavily. "Less than enthusiastic about bonding with me."

"Take care of your mate first, son. Justice doesn't come with a time restriction, but a mate's heart is something you can't put off for later. This one is special, I can feel it."

Manning leaned back in his chair and narrowed his gaze on his father. "You've been talking to Merebeth."

"Maybe."

"And you're not going to tell me any more than she or George has."

"Not a word."

He shook his head and rose from the table. "As much as I love having these cryptic talks, I can think of a few better things to do with my time. Bye, Dad."

"George dropped your car off this morning, by the way. Said as long as you're going to be hanging around his place, you might as well make yourself useful and help out with his truck. He can do with an extra set of tools and hands."

"Of course he can." Manning waved to his father then grabbed his tools from the garage and loaded them into his car. Assisting George was actually the perfect excuse to spend time around Quinn, even if he had no illusions that the older shifter really would put him to work.

Chapter Five

In town, he stopped by the pet store, recalling something Quinn had told him the night before, and loaded a container holding a small box turtle into the car. As he pulled into Merebeth's driveway, George came around from the side of the house and waved him over.

"You can see him in a few hours when they break for lunch. Did you bring the tools?"

Manning set his tools and the present for Quinn on the ground beside the truck. "Yeah, and thanks for driving my car back. Did you talk to Merebeth after she calmed Quinn down last night?"

"I tried not to, but she forced me anyway. Relax, your boy's fine. Made of tougher stuff than that. He'd have to be to work with my mate. Now grab a wrench and that sliding board over there and let's get dirty."

Manning rolled his eyes, and his sleeves, then got to work under the truck. At around midday, Merebeth came out with a glass of lemonade for George, and told Manning one was waiting for him in the kitchen. Manning grinned when she winked at him, thankful beyond measure she didn't hold last night's disaster against him. After gathering his present, he walked into the house and took a deep breath, picking up the scent of his mate and following it to the kitchen. Quinn stood at the table with a cup halfway to his mouth and a book held about six inches from his face.

Manning paused in the doorway to admire the sight before him, watching the way the man's lips moved with each word that he read. After several seconds, Quinn breathed in deeply and looked up, a slight smile curving his mouth before it quickly turned to a frown.

"What are you doing here?"

Unaffected by the candid question, Manning walked to his mate and placed a kiss on Quinn's cheek before the man could object and took his book and mug to put on the table. "It's nice to see you, too. And why wouldn't I be here?"

Quinn shrugged and looked away. "I thought after what happened, you'd come to your senses."

"I'll try not to take that as an insinuation that I'm not in my right mind." He pushed his mate into a chair then took the one next to it and slid his present across the table. "I got something for you."

"Don't you have work to do?"

"Yeah, and George is a slave driver, so I doubt I'll have much time for lunch. Open the box."

Quinn stared at him suspiciously, then at the package. With hesitant hands, he opened it and looked inside, then gently picked up the animal within. "A turtle?" Doubt colored his voice, but that smile returned as he put the turtle in his palm and petted the underside of its chin with one finger.

"You told me your mind has a tendency of running away with you when it starts crunching numbers. I thought having this little guy around would help slow it down some." His stomach flipped as Quinn's smile grew. "He's a bit old, but the woman at the store told me he's real friendly."

Quinn nodded and brought the turtle up to peer at its face. "Old and slow. Every time I see him I'll think of you."

Manning couldn't help but laugh as his mate gave him a mischievous grin. "Thanks. I'll remember that when I get your next present."

The smile slowly faded from Quinn's face as he put the turtle down. "This isn't going to work."

"Because of what happened last night?"

Quinn stood and raked a hand through his hair. "Because of everything. I think you know by now that I have issues. We're from two completely different worlds and you're not even gay!"

Manning stood as well and stalked after his mate, who'd retreated to the other side of the room. "I don't have to be gay to know that I'm attracted to you. I'll build a bridge every day to cross this divide you see between us, and there isn't a person alive that doesn't have issues. Hell, I've got so many I'd have gray hairs if I weren't a shifter."

His mate was backed up against the counter, staring up at him in shock, but he couldn't restrain his next words. "Yes, I have a job to do and duties to attend, but I happen to think you're more important than them. You're my mate, but more than that, you're someone I want to get to know, and unless you tell me to leave, I'm not going anywhere." He put his hands on the counter on either side of his mate, effectively trapping but not touching him. Quinn was flushed and panting lightly, but no cloying scent of fear wafted from his skin.

Crimson Mate

"I stop working at five."

Manning blinked, not quite sure he'd heard right. "Are you inviting me over for dinner?"

A spark glittered in Quinn's eyes. "You were the one who said you wanted to get know me better. You don't..."

Manning shut his mate's mouth with a kiss. Joy twined its way through his chest and he wanted nothing more than to continue what they'd started the night before but held back. "Tonight sounds great. Don't forget to eat lunch. There's food in the box for the turtle." He gave Quinn one more kiss then went outside to where George was waiting for him. The other man handed him one of two plates stacked with sandwiches and chips, which Manning took gratefully.

George grunted and shook his head. "Merebeth figured you'd forget to grab food for yourself. Hurry and eat. I want to get as much labor out of you as I can before the sun goes down."

And he did. By the time five o'clock rolled around, they were both covered in sweat and grease, and were ready to call it a day. Manning wiped off his tools and added them to George's collection in the garage on the other side of the cottage. After waving goodbye to the man, he drove to his house where he showered and shaved in record time. On the way back, he dug his vibrating cell phone from his pants pocket and frowned at the unknown number.

After pressing the send button, he said, "Manning."

"Hi."

"Quinn?"

"Yeah, sorry. Merebeth gave me your number."

Manning smiled at the lilting cadence of his mate's voice. "Don't apologize, baby. I should've

71

remembered to give it to you yesterday." When there was a short pause, he asked, "Quinn?"

"Umm, can you pick up a pizza?"

"Sure, but I can cook something there. I don't mind."

"No, that's really not necessary. I like pepperoni. I'll, uh, I'll see you soon."

Manning frowned again as the line went dead. Okay, pizza it was. After programming the number into his phone, he headed back into town and picked up a pizza, as well as anything else he thought his mate might like. Thirty minutes later, Quinn answered his door a little distractedly and waved him in. The odor of burnt food hit Manning immediately as he followed Quinn into the kitchen, noticing that every window in the small apartment was open.

"Is everything all right?"

Quinn grumbled something unintelligible and walked to the sink where he began scrubbing at a pan within. Manning put the food boxes on the counter then went to his mate who was studiously ignoring him. He pulled Quinn's hands from the water, turned him around and tilted his chin up with two fingers. "What happened?"

Quinn blew a lock of hair from his eyes and said, "I was trying to make you dinner but apparently you can't leave dead chicken unattended. It died a horrible death and Merebeth said my kitchen needs at least a day to recuperate before I try cooking anything else."

It took all that he had to hold in the laughter that threatened to burst from his chest. Quinn was truly agitated, and from what Manning had gathered about him thus far, the man couldn't stand to make mistakes. "Thank you. It means a lot that you tried to cook for me."

"It does?"

Manning stared down at the uncertainty in his mate's soft, gray eyes. What would it take to replace that look with confidence and trust? "Yes, but I've been craving pizza all day, so this works out even better."

Quinn's lips curved up in a slow grin. "No you weren't."

"Are you kidding? I practically live off the stuff. Come on. Let's eat before it gets cold." He released his mate to search for plates and napkins.

"I thought you liked to cook."

"I said I can. Never said I was fond of it."

Quinn chuckled as he poured soda for them. After filling their plates, they moved to the living room where Quinn put on one of his few movies to which neither paid attention. They sat on the couch and talked about their day until the conversation gravitated toward Manning. His life, his past and current position. How he governed his people and what each community was like.

Quinn's eagerness to know everything about him and their kind was invigorating, same as it had been on their first date, but Manning couldn't help but notice his mate was avoiding answering questions about his own past. Just as he also noticed that almost nothing in the living room or kitchen belonged to Quinn. All of the personal touches and decorations, including the furniture, were things Manning had seen before in Merebeth's house. The most intimate piece of knowledge he'd managed to glean from his mate so far was that he had an older sister who also lived in the States and a brother with whom he no longer spoke.

As soon as there was a pause, Manning asked, "How long did you live in France?"

Quinn looked away then got up to put another movie in. "It doesn't matter. I'm here now."

"It matters to me. I want to know."

With a huff, Quinn sent him a frustrated glare. "Why?"

"Because your past is part of what makes you who you are and I want to get to know all of you." Manning kept his expression neutral as Quinn worried at his bottom lip as though struggling with an internal debate. Several tense seconds later, Quinn sat back down on the couch but kept his gaze on the TV.

"I was born and raised there. I moved to the United States with my sister three years ago."

"It must have been hard growing up so close to our enemy."

Quinn looked at him. "You mean the *Vam'kir?*"

"Of course."

"They are not the enemy," he said with sudden vehemence. "Not all of them."

Manning turned to face his mate fully. "Quinn, I know you weren't raised in a shifter community, but the *Vam'kir* have been our enemy for centuries. They've started wars and killed hundreds of our kind."

"And you've—*we've*—killed just as many of theirs. Most of them only try to defend themselves. They have schools and clans full of families just trying to survive. Many of them were my friends when I was growing up."

Anger thickened Manning's voice as he growled, "Your parents should never have put you at risk like that."

"My parents were assholes, but it wasn't because of who I grew up with. The *Vam'kir* never hurt me. Not until…"

The same haunted look Manning had seen last night darkened Quinn's eyes and his body began to shake. "Not until you matured," he finished. "*Vam'kir* can only sense us once our spirits mature."

"That was different."

"They could have killed you."

Quinn jumped up, fists clenched at his sides. "It wasn't their fault, it was mine!" He stormed from the room to the back of the apartment, leaving Manning to sit in stunned silence.

Eventually, rage began to burn its way through his veins like acid, but it wasn't directed at his mate. His anger was reserved for the fools who had not only put their children's lives at risk, but also apparently told Quinn that it was his fault, as if he'd had a choice in the maturing of his spirit. Hands clenched at his sides, he willed his riotous emotions under control and went after his mate. He found him in the bedroom staring out of the window and slowly walked over but kept a distance of a few feet between them.

Quinn turned, his eyes shining determinedly. "You are the *Jaes'din*. Born with the power to command your entire race. They depend on you to lead them. How can you do that without truly knowing your *enemy*? The *Vam'kir* love and work and fight to survive just like the *Ba'Kal* do. What makes them so different from you?"

"Don't you mean 'us'?"

Quinn drew his brows down. "Us. Them. We've all committed crimes and retaliated. No one knows who started the war between the races but neither side has done anything to stop it. Why do you hate them when shifters behave no differently than trancers?"

"They killed my mother," he ground out.

Compassion softened his mate's features. "I'm sorry. No one should have to deal with that kind of pain." After several seconds, Quinn placed a hand on Manning's arm, holding his gaze intently. "Tell me it's okay to condemn an entire race and I will."

Manning opened his mouth, the words on the tip of his tongue, but nothing came out. He took a step back, feeling as though the world had tilted on its axis. All his life, he'd been trained in the ways of his enemy. Their fighting techniques, locations and language. Stories abounded of their cruelty in and out of war, yet could he really say that his kind was any less aggressive? There was no doubt the innocent trancers the Alphas had found had been murdered. Had they deserved to die for an injustice they hadn't committed merely because they were considered the enemy?

In retrospect, he'd always known that not all trancers were warriors, but he'd never considered the perspective Quinn was throwing at him. In all honesty, he could no more blame the families of those innocent trancers for hating his race than he could the families of his own kind who had suffered needlessly. Violence begat violence, but as the *Jaes'din*, how far was he willing to take it, and where did it end?

"You're right. I can't condemn all trancers for the acts of a few, but I will get revenge for my mother's murder."

"On the ones who are responsible."

Manning smiled at his mate's tenacity. "Yes, only on the ones who deserve it, once I find them."

"How long ago has it been?"

"Two months. I've already sent men to track them, but they were unsuccessful."

"So when will you leave to search for them yourself?"

A deep breath filled his lungs as he braced himself for the admission. "As soon as I know I won't lose you."

Quinn started, shaken by the sincerity in Manning's tone. He wanted to laugh, call the man an outright liar, a fool. But he'd seen, he'd *felt*, what it had cost Manning to swallow his pride and admit he was wrong about all trancers, especially in the face of his grief over the death of a parent—both parents—if Manning's father followed his mate. Another tradition their races shared.

The man was telling the truth, but it was built on a lie.

He cleared his throat and whispered, "Excuse me," before all but running from the room. In the bathroom, he closed the door and splashed cold water on his face. A glance in the mirror showed the turmoil burning within. Born of the royal family of *Vam'kir*, he knew exactly how much hatred and deception was bred into shifters and trancers alike. When he'd challenged Manning's convictions, he'd fully expected to be castigated. This would've given him all the reason he needed to end everything right then. He could never learn to love someone who hated a part of him.

Only, that hadn't been the case. Manning had relented to his argument, proving there was room for change. But would his acceptance still hold true if he ever discovered his mate was a trancer?

Did Quinn really want to find out?

With a sigh, he turned off the light then walked back to his room, and stopped. Manning looked up at him from the open pad he was holding in one hand then turned it around for Quinn to see. It was the drawing he'd sketched on the first day they'd seen each other, the one that was supposed to be hidden from view in the bottom drawer of the nightstand.

"Why did you run from me that day, Quinn?" When no response was forthcoming, he tossed the pad onto the bed then strode forward with purpose. "What happened last night that scared you?" Manning stepped closer still to caress his cheek then gently brace the back of his neck. "Answer one or the other. I don't care which, but let me have one. I need to know."

The decision was immediate. If he answered the first question, it was sure to lead to a slew of others he wasn't ready to deal with yet, but that wasn't why he chose to respond to the second. Chills danced along his skin as his mouth went dry. Every nerve ending in his body reacted to the electrifying touch of the man, his scent and overwhelming presence. Quinn couldn't think past the promise of tenderness in the depths of Manning's dark gaze. He wanted it, needed it, and the answer he provided might give it to him.

"Canines."

Manning's forehead creased in confusion. "What?"

With a slight pause to gather his courage, he said, "Your canines. When they dropped, it reminded me of...something else." Someone else, but he wouldn't elaborate.

Manning sighed and pulled him into a fierce hug. "I could kill whoever hurt you before you came here."

The thought of Manning confronting the tormentor of his past caused a shudder to wrack him. "I'm here now."

The large man pulled back to look down at him. "Yes, you are."

Desire pounded through him as Manning's mouth slanted across his. The touch was soft, sensuous, and when a moist tongue flicked across the seam of his lips, seeking entrance, he opened with a low moan. Long fingers threaded through his hair and tilted his head back. Quinn shivered as Manning deepened the kiss and walked him backward until he hit the wall behind him. The crush of the man's hard body against his caused adrenaline to spike through his system. The feel of so much coiled strength surrounding him and sliding along his smaller frame was both thrilling and intimidating.

With Sean, everything had been new and exciting. They'd fumbled their way through the discoveries of their likes and dislikes and those experiences had only added to the pleasures they'd found with each other. They had been equals in their hunger and naivety, and nothing had felt more right.

During the long, bleak years afterward, he'd learned what it was to live on the other side of that spectrum, and how it felt to be stripped of all control and dominated both physically and mentally. The memory of Sean was all that had kept him going through the nightmare that his life had become. The harshest reality he'd had to face during his recovery, however, had been that what he'd had with Sean could never be recaptured.

But he wasn't sure he wanted it to be anymore.

Manning was unlike anything he'd previously known. He was hesitant yet possessive, gentle yet dominant, all at once. The contrasts created an unexpected balance that invoked a feeling of power within Quinn and, at the same time, had him yearning to surrender.

Quinn gasped when Manning lifted him with two splayed hands on his ass. As he wrapped his legs around the man's tapered waist, the feel of an unyielding length against his sent ripples of fire blazing across his flesh. Manning rocked his hips again and again, grinding their erections together until the friction had Quinn nearly mad with lust. Quinn laughed breathlessly between the merciless swipes of the man's questing tongue. The loss of control felt so unbelievably good, to let go of his inhibitions and allow his desire to flow through him.

Manning spun them around and Quinn yelped as he was tossed onto the bed. In the next instant, the heat of Manning's body returned to envelop him and push him down into the mattress. The heavy weight incited a flicker of apprehension, but it quickly dissipated as piercing, golden eyes met his. Naked desire shone in their brilliant depths but no insanity.

"Okay so far, pup?"

Quinn smiled at the endearment. It somehow brought their worlds closer and made him feel like he belonged instead of being an outsider. At his nod, Manning lifted the hem of Quinn's shirt and pulled it off.

"Damn, you're sexy," Manning growled.

Insecurity flared and before he could think better of it, he blurted, "How would you know? You've never been with a guy."

Manning sat up and blinked, then let out a throaty laugh. "Our kind may be able to shift forms while clothed," his lips skimmed down Quinn's chest then bathed one nipple in the heat of his mouth, "but we have no reservations about nudity." He sucked in and bit the hardened nub, rolling it between his teeth. "I've seen plenty of naked men in my life, and none of them compare to you." He repeated the process to the other nipple and raked his nails lightly down Quinn's abs to the waistband of his pants. "Or perhaps you'd like me to come back after I have a little more experience?"

Jealousy ripped through Quinn and he latched onto the man's skull, dragging him up to take possession of his mouth. His spirit spurred him on as he delved inside and drank greedily of Manning's intoxicating taste. "I am your mate," he said with a ferociousness that shocked him into immobility in the next instant.

What the hell did I just say? But then there was no time to think. Manning's lips were on him again, his hands sliding and grasping until Quinn realized they were beneath the cover of his pants. Without thought, he raised his pelvis to allow the larger man to yank the material away.

"Wait—" but his protest was cut off as Manning gripped his aching member in a strong fist. Shimmering, yellow irises flashed up at him through thick fringes and fixed him with a compelling stare.

"Relax for me, baby. I won't take this any further than you're ready to go."

Quinn's mind was still reeling from the words that had tumbled out unbidden, but he found himself nodding and melting into the man's confident hold. That is until Manning opened up to engulf the head of his cock in searing heat. His hips surged up of their own accord, driving half of his length into the cavern of Manning's mouth. The man set up a vigorous pace, pumping Quinn's straining cock with his lips and stroking his clenched hand in a counter motion that squeezed every inch and had Quinn writhing beneath him.

Manning began to swallow more and more of him with each pass so that soon, only a finger and thumb were circled tightly around the base. The suction increased around his throbbing length and he could feel the storm of his orgasm building, spiraling rapidly out of control. He reached up to the headboard above to keep from forcing the man's head farther down.

"I'm gonna... I can't stop," he said, panting with the effort to take in air.

Manning pulled away to moisten one of his fingers then dove right back down. One of his thick arms banded around Quinn's waist to hold him down while the other snaked beneath one of his legs. When the tip of the slicked finger rubbed along his quivering entrance and pushed in, his climax bowled through him with unrelenting speed. Quinn cried out as his body jerked with spasms and muscles convulsed around the head of his cock to milk him dry until he was trembling with the aftermath of his release.

It had been so long, too long, since his body had succumbed to the pleasure of another's touch without force or coercion. Quinn felt as though he would sink through the bed if not for the firm hands holding him and moving up his body. Soft lips once more molded to his and he moaned at the combination of Manning's unique flavor and that of his own cum. A deep, rumbling laugh vibrated his tongue then disappeared along with the comforting weight of the man above him.

"Go to sleep, pup. I'll see you in the morning."

Quinn squinted up through heavy lids and grabbed onto Manning's shirt before he could leave. *Don't go*, he wanted to say, but the words stuck in his constricted throat. He knew Manning was leaving to give him space and, honestly, he needed time to sort through the kaleidoscope of his emotions, yet he didn't want the man to go. Manning had just made him feel what he'd thought forever lost to him, but what would happen if he asked Manning to stay? Would the man see that as a sign of submission and demand more? Oddly, that idea didn't bother Quinn nearly as much as it should have.

Manning smiled, brushed a damp lock of hair from Quinn's forehead then kissed it. "I'll be right outside."

The last thing Quinn remembered was the press of his blanket being tucked around his body and the quiet pad of Manning's retreating footsteps.

Chapter Six

On the other side of the window pane, sleek, sweat-drenched muscles bunched and stretched like a visual symphony in the bright afternoon sunlight. Manning was wearing only blue cutoffs and a sleeveless, white T-shirt that clung to his broad chest. His tanned skin glistened like a painted canvas sprinkled by an aged scotch, just begging to be licked dry.

Quinn ground his teeth but couldn't tear his gaze away from the vision outside. Three days had passed since Manning had touched him with more than a simple hug, a caress on the cheek, a lingering kiss. He knew why, but instead of comforting him, the man's patience was driving him insane. The least Manning could do was make a move so that he could brush him off, or accept it, or something! But no. He was waiting on Quinn to take the initiative.

And why the hell do I care? Again, he knew why, but that didn't make it any easier to unravel his tangled feelings. Every day he was met with opportunities to rid himself of the man, but it was he who invited Manning in every evening for dinner. He who kept him company at lunch and gazed into those vibrant, yellow eyes in the darkness of the forest's edge before going to bed each night. Their relationship was progressing into a two-sided affair he couldn't quite to get enough of.

When he was with Manning, nothing else seemed to matter. Not the blood in his veins or the violence of his past, or even the fact that they never went out. If the man was discontent in any way, he never let it show.

"Hey, lover boy, you might want to peel your eyeballs away from the window candy long enough to answer your phone."

Quinn jerked at the sound of Merebeth's voice. "What?"

She gave him a lopsided, knowing grin and pointed to his phone on the footstool in front of him. "It's gone off twice now, Mr Popularity."

With a mumbled thanks, he picked up his cell phone and checked the missed calls. *Shit!* He'd completely forgotten he was supposed to pick up Cassie from the airport. Today was the first day of the full moon and, as promised, she'd flown in to provide him with the blood he needed to survive. Mara, he'd been told, would go with Shannon to find humans to trance since she had classes she couldn't miss. He jumped up and ran to his apartment for his keys while dialing her back.

"Well it's about time, stranger. I was beginning to think you didn't love me anymore."

"I'm so sorry! Am I late? I'm headed into town now," he said with a guilty wince.

Cassie's tinkling laughter spilled through the small speaker. "It's all right. I decided to rent a car since you don't have room for me at your place and I'll go stir crazy if I'm stuck at a hotel all day. I'd have told you earlier, but *somebody* kept me up late last night and I almost missed my flight this morning."

Quinn breathed a sigh of relief and chuckled. "How is Mara doing?"

"Oh, you know, it's finals week and she was using me to take her stress out on. Not that I mind. My baby can get pretty wicked when she wants to. Last night, she tied me to the bed and used her teeth to—"

"Cassie!"

"Aw, you're blushing, aren't you? Damn, and I promised myself I'd wait to tell you so I could see you squirm. Anyway, she's sorry she couldn't come as well. Listen, I'm getting my car now. There's supposed to be this awesome café downtown called Perk It Up. Know where it is?"

No, but Merebeth was bound to. "Yeah."

"Good. I'll meet you there. Ciao, babe."

He ended the call with a grin then got directions from Merebeth after telling her he'd be back by nightfall. Merebeth waved goodbye, fully informed of what he had planned after their discussion the night before, then went back to glaring at the numbers on her laptop. Outside, he hesitated on the porch, not sure if he should tell Manning he was leaving, but the choice was made for him when the man called him over to George's pickup.

Manning wiped his hands on a rag then took both of Quinn's hands in his and studied them. "Yep, you'll do fine. George dropped a tool down in the engine and my hands are too big to reach in and get it. Think you can climb up there and get it out?"

Quinn looked around, noting that George was nowhere in sight. He didn't really have time but found he couldn't say no either. "Okay, where is it?"

"All the way to the back. Here, let me help you up."

He stepped onto the bumper and pulled himself up, with Manning holding him steady by the hips. The engine was layered in dirt and grease, making it hard to see into the deep crevices.

"I don't see anything."

"Lean forward more. That's it. Up a little farther."

"Are you sure it didn't drop on the ground?"

"Bend down so you can get a closer look. There you go. Very nice."

Quinn froze at Manning's rough tone and twisted around to peer over his shoulder. Manning was staring straight at his ass, blatant lust shining from his eyes. "There is no tool in here, is there?"

Manning glanced from Quinn to the bottom in front of him and back again. "There is if you want there to be," he said in a voice several octaves lower.

Heat scalded his cheeks, but he couldn't keep in the burst of laughter that came out. Nor the flare of arousal that shot through him. Manning flirted with him constantly and Quinn was learning to recognize the sexual innuendos as compliments rather than threats. This was an addictive boost to the ego, to say the least.

As he was scooting back out, his shoe slipped on the bumper and only Manning's quick reflexes saved him from tumbling to the ground. Quinn felt his breath catch as he was caught and pulled up against the large man, chest to chest. The craving in Manning's eyes hadn't diminished one iota as they stood staring at each other for long seconds.

Quinn cleared his throat and managed to get out, "I have to go."

"Where?"

"My sister's girlfriend came to visit. I'm going to meet her."

Manning grinned widely. "Perfect timing. I could use a break. We'll take my car."

"No," he said a little too hastily. "I mean, it'll probably be boring for you and I won't be long."

Manning's brow furrowed slightly. "You haven't told them about me yet." This wasn't a question, and Quinn didn't answer. "It's okay, baby. They're going to find out sooner or later. Might as well be now."

Well, fuck. This could get bad, or really, really bad. There was no way he could let Manning watch him drink from Cassie, and if his arousal flared while any other shifters were near, as it often did in the man's presence, he might have to run for his life again. Another dead giveaway that he was different.

"Quinn," Manning said sternly, "I can't let you go alone. You don't have to introduce me as your boyfriend, but there's been some trouble lately and I'd feel better if I were with you."

Quinn stifled a huff of frustration and relented. It was the first time, apart from the day they'd met, that the man had aggressively insinuated himself into Quinn's life, which meant the danger he was alluding to was probably very real. The situation was definitely going to call for some smooth finagling.

During the trip into town, Quinn filled Manning in with as much detail as he dared on his relationship with Cassie, which wasn't much more than he'd already revealed. At the coffee shop, Cassie spotted him from inside and ran out to meet him. Within moments, his arms were full of bouncing, ecstatic, blonde happiness. He hugged her back just as tightly. Mara's scent was still mingled in with the woman's natural fragrance, causing a feeling of homesickness to wash over him.

"I can't believe how much I've missed you! And you look so good. I brought my camera so we can take...pictures..." She drew back slowly, taking in Manning's huge form standing a short distance away. "And who might this be? Friend of yours?"

Quinn looked back at the Manning, who quirked an eyebrow at him. Could it really hurt to tell the truth? Okay, partial truth. Cassie couldn't tell that the man was a shifter and, Cassie being human, Manning wouldn't be volunteering any unnecessary information.

"This is my boyfriend, Manning. Manning, this is Cassie."

Cassie's eyes bulged as she gaped inelegantly. "Oh, my God. He's... He's..." Turning to Quinn, she asked, "Does he...?"

Quinn shook his head to confirm that Manning didn't know he was a trancer.

Manning frowned. "Do I what?"

"Swing both ways," Cassie said without skipping a beat. "He's gorgeous!" She threw herself at a confused Manning and wrapped him in a crushing hug. "I can't wait to tell Mara. She's going to flip!"

With teeth clamped down on the inside of his cheek to suppress a grimace, Quinn led the way into the café where they sat down to eat. An hour later, he got his first real look at the town as Cassie insisted they show her the highlights, of which there weren't many. Throughout the day, he noticed they hadn't encountered a single shifter. When he pulled Manning to the side to ask about it, he was told most shifters in the area preferred to stay within the community close by.

Their reticence to interact unnecessarily with humans made sense, and certainly made things a lot easier, but it was still difficult for him to keep his composure around so many people. He'd only just begun to venture out into public again when he'd first seen Manning. After seven years of seclusion, he'd grown accustomed to it. Despite his effort to relax, it didn't take long for Manning to pick up on his increasing agitation, but instead of commenting on it, he merely found other ways to keep Quinn's mind occupied such as holding his hand, touching his back and, to Quinn's embarrassment, kissing him whenever the mood seemed to strike him. Which was often.

Is this what it would be like if we were bonded? Quinn couldn't help but wonder, and dream.

By evening, they stopped by a grocery store to pick up food supplies for Cassie then drove to the hotel where she was staying. When they pulled up, Quinn still hadn't thought of an excuse to get away from Manning but, again, Cassie had him covered.

"Would you mind if I talked to Quinny for a bit in private? I've got some family problems I need to discuss with him that are a little personal."

"Sure," Manning replied, though it was obvious he wasn't too pleased about it.

Quinn smiled awkwardly then got out of the car to follow Cassie to her room. Once inside, the excitement she'd apparently held in during the day exploded from her in a burst of bubbling exuberance.

"He's amazing! I can't believe it. Your first time dating in years and you find a hunk like that, and he's such a gentleman. Did you see the way he opened every door for you?"

"Yeah, I was there," he mumbled.

"What's wrong? Is it...? Oh, babe, if you're not ready to have sex yet, just tell him. He seems like he'd understand and you've only known him for less than a week. Anyone worth it will wait for you."

Quinn only nodded as he went to the small refrigerating unit, took from it a bottle of orange juice and water and set both on the dresser for Cassie. Manning wasn't the one who caused him to worry, it was *him*. Logically, he knew he had to end the farce of a relationship he had with the man. This sham of a prelude to something better, something lifelong, wasn't fair. Manning deserved a person who didn't have to deceive, lie and pretend to be something he wasn't just to live a shell of a life. He deserved love, not a mate who could never bond with him because the sight of fangs causes him to have a mental breakdown. Canines were slightly broader, thicker and duller than fangs, but close enough in appearance.

"Hey." Cassie pulled him from his reverie with a soft caress on his cheek. "It'll be okay, little brother. Just don't give up."

Quinn smiled and knelt on the floor by the side of the bed. Cassie kicked off her shoes, pulled back the covers then sat beside him on the mattress. Her delicate wrist seemed so fragile in his hand as he lifted it to his mouth and concentrated on the unique, sweet scent of her blood and the sound of it being pumped through her veins by the steady palpating of her heart. With the added allure of the full moon waiting to shine in the night sky, the compulsive need to feed rose, sharp and undeniable. His fangs dropped with sudden urgency and his gut clenched painfully, but he pierced her skin as gently as possible and drank in smooth, shallow pulls.

When he'd taken enough to get him through the night, he retracted his fangs and licked the puncture wounds until they sealed shut. The healing agents in his saliva weren't strong, but they were enough to prevent further bleeding and infection. Carefully, he eased her back on the bed, pulled the covers up around her slight frame and gave her a kiss.

Cassie smiled sleepily. "Love you, Quinny."

With a silent prayer of thanks to the Mother for giving his sister such a wonderful mate, he returned the sentiment and left quietly.

The sun was just sinking past the horizon by the time they arrived back at Merebeth's. Quinn opened the door to his apartment and turned to Manning for their customary goodnight kiss but paused when he saw the man fidgeting.

"Is something wrong?"

"No," Manning shook his head, "but I was wondering if you wanted to run with me tonight. Merebeth said you didn't have plans to go with her and George."

Quinn gripped the knob of the door, turning to hide the anger seething inside. *What the hell had she been thinking?* Stupid question. He knew exactly what she was up to, but this time she'd gone too far. Tonight was to be the night of his first shift. He'd been fighting it, and had been able to because of his *Vam'kir* blood, since his spirit had matured. Merebeth had agreed to aid him with the change, but she'd obviously pawned him off on Manning in the hopes it would help their relationship progress.

How could he tell Manning he'd never shifted before without raising suspicion?

He couldn't. Manning was smart. He'd figure out that there was something different about Quinn that enabled him to deny the change when it was nearly physically impossible for any normal shifter to do so. Quinn would lose him.

Pain lanced through him, taking his breath away.

There was always the option of sending Manning away and going to Merebeth for help regardless of her scheming, but he was too angry to face her. This night and the next would just have to be like every other monthly cycle of the moon. He would deal with the agony of denial alone where no one could witness it.

"Quinn?"

"I can't go with you tonight." He went in and pushed the door closed, but Manning stopped it with his boot.

"What's wrong?"

Quinn scowled over his shoulder at the authoritative note in Manning's voice and kept walking. "Run with your pack, Manning. I don't want to go with you." Maybe if he was harsh enough, the man would leave him be.

He didn't.

"Tell me what's going on."

"We're not bonded. I don't have to tell you, so get out!"

Quinn gasped as he was whipped around and shoved into the hallway wall. Manning's palm on his chest seared through the material of his shirt. He should be scared, but he wasn't. The predatory look blazing in the other man's dark eyes ignited a spark of pleasure that jolted through his body as chills pricked his skin and his cock swelled to near pain. Not once, *not once,* had he enjoyed his years of forced submission. But this was... *Fuck!* Fierce control emanated from Manning's posture, his very being, yet it was tempered with something that made Quinn's heart clench and his gut tighten.

The man was glorious in his dominance. Even then, with Manning bearing down on him, Quinn knew he was safe, maybe even cared for.

Manning leaned down so that their faces were only inches apart. "Tell me."

"I've never shifted," Quinn rasped through the dryness of his throat.

"What?" Manning's hand went slack and dropped to his side.

Desire instantly cooled in the wake of his admission. "I don't want to talk about it. Please, just go." He turned to move away but was stopped by a hand on his arm.

"Wait. Denying the change is dangerous. Many shifters have died from the pain of trying. I can keep myself from shifting with only minor discomfort, but that's because I'm the *Jaes'din*. Are you telling me you've suffered through every full moon for the past seven years?"

Quinn gave him a blank stare.

"Is it a genetic defect? Are you...part human?" Manning looked around then back at him as though grasping at straws. "Have...? Have you been doing this to yourself as some sort of punishment for something?"

"No!" His father would have killed him had he given in to the shift instead of only beating him unconscious every month.

"Someone did this to you. Damn it!"

Quinn jerked as Manning punched a hole through the wall opposite him. Terror flooded in and he turned to run but was stopped again when Manning gripped both of his arms.

"I'm sorry." After visibly collecting himself, he said, "Forgive me. It just scares me to think of how close I might have come to losing you." He pulled Quinn into the circle of his arms, bent his head down and growled, "Please tell me the asshole that did this is still alive."

Warmth seeped into Quinn's trembling body, chasing away his momentary fear. He nodded against the man's broad chest and grinned secretively at the words that came next.

"Good. When you trust me enough to tell me who it is, I'll kill him." On a deep, indrawn breath, Manning kissed the crown of his head then tilted it back so that their eyes met. "Will you let me help you through tonight?"

Quinn frowned. That was it? No interminable questions, no accusations or even a hint of suspicion?

Manning passed a thumb lightly over his lips. "I don't need to know everything right now. You'll tell me when you're ready."

While Quinn shook his head, he felt a small smile tug at his lips. The man was infuriating in his persistence, stubbornness and charm. At every turn, he was given ample reason to leave, yet here he stood with calm patience and unfathomable trust. Everyone had flaws, even Manning, but right then Quinn couldn't see them past the sincerity in his eyes. "Perfection will get you nowhere."

"I'll have to work on that," Manning said around a growing grin. "Do you have any liquor?"

"I have wine left over—"

"Not good enough. We're gonna need the hard stuff for this. Come on." He led Quinn to the living room and pushed him down onto the couch. "I know where Merebeth hides her stash. Give me two minutes."

Quinn watched the man stride from the apartment, too dazed to do anything but sit and wait for his return, which didn't take long. Manning came back and placed a fifth of bourbon and several shot glasses he'd pilfered from Merebeth's house onto the floor, moved the coffee table aside then began to remove every piece of clothing from his body.

"Umm... What are you doing?"

"Strip."

Yeah. That might be possible if he could remember how to move. Hard ridges of muscles rippled beneath bronze-colored skin as Manning stretched and bent, revealing every inch of his firm body. His movements were as graceful and elegant as those of the panther Quinn had admired from his window each night before going to sleep. A light dusting of black hairs traveled from Manning's sleek chest down to a slim line that ended in a trim patch of pubic hair. The generous member that hung loosely between his legs began to slowly stiffen and curve upward, rocking from side to side as he advanced toward the couch.

Quinn's mouth went dry again as Manning knelt in front of him and quirked one corner of his mouth up seductively.

"Get undressed."

Was he out of his fucking mind? With a snort, Quinn responded, "No."

"I've seen you naked."

"I'm happy for you." He crossed his arms over his skinny chest and cursed silently as understanding lit the other man's eyes.

Manning furrowed his brow in a contemplative frown then sat back on his haunches. "I could sit here all night and tell you how sexy you are and you'd never believe me. You think too much. Fortunately, I have a remedy for that." From the floor, he began filling all five of the glasses with liquor. "Drink this," he said, proffering one of the shots. When Quinn hesitated, he glanced at the clock on the wall. "The sun has set and the moon is rising. We don't have much time."

Quinn took the glass but paused with it at his lips. "How do I know you're not just trying to take advantage of me?"

"Baby, I've been trying to do that since I met you. However, Merebeth would have my balls on a platter if I did that now and I happen to like where they are."

The man had a point. Quinn downed the shot then coughed as fire scorched his insides. Manning took the empty glass and handed him another.

"The first shift is always painful, not only because your body is adjusting to the change, but your mind is as well. When our spirit comes to us at birth, it is essentially its own being, separate from us yet a part of us." He brought the second glass to Quinn's lips and upended it, waiting until the liquid was swallowed before replacing it with more. "Upon maturity, we're forced to join with it and, contrary to popular belief among pups, that melding of souls and minds does not come easily. In fact, both the shifter and the spirit try to reject one another."

Quinn shook his head against another shot, but Manning persisted by tipping the glass at his mouth, other hand firmly on the nape of his neck, and won.

"Right now you can feel your spirit, hear it, but the shift will fuse the two of you together in a bond that will run deeper than any of your senses. The two become one, and I promise that once it happens, you'll feel complete."

"Then why are you getting me drunk?" Quinn tried to slump back, but Manning was there to hold him up. He shivered as the man's hands reached beneath his shirt and tugged it over his head.

"Like I said, the initial shift isn't easy. It's a natural battle for dominance between two rebellious souls that need to realize that they work better in tandem than they ever will separately. The liquor dulls our reactions and makes it easier for our bodies to accept what our minds are too stubborn to yield to. That and it helps with the pain. Your body will burn it out of your system by the time the shift is complete."

Quinn lifted his ass, belatedly noticing that Manning was pulling his pants and underwear off, his shoes already having disappeared.

"Take one more."

Batting half-heartedly at the fourth glass, he chuckled and fell into Manning's lap with a wave of dizziness. "You're so fullovit. But sssexy," he slurred. Damn, he'd never felt so good, or happy. Manning made him happy. He didn't know why he kept the man at a distance. Maybe... "Ungh." The sharp stab of familiar pain knifed through his gut.

"Quinn, take the shot."

He tried to push away, but Manning held him tightly. This was wrong. He couldn't do this. "No."

"Baby, don't fight it. Let your spirit in."

Cramps rolled through his belly as a piercing throb beat at his temples. His father's words began to echo in the back of his mind, taunting him and growing in volume until they competed with the vehemence in Manning's voice. The past came back with a vengeance to soak his thoughts, spilling into his mind and carrying with it the litany of his father's hatred.

'I should've known you were no son of mine. Weak and pathetic, worse than those filthy animals who have the audacity to worship the Mother. You're nothing but an abomination.'

Quinn whimpered and struggled against the arms that held him, recalling the fetid stench of his small cell and the blistering pain of his father's belt splitting open his naked flesh.

'Don't you dare shift in my house! I won't let you taint my walls with your perversion. You think this is pain? It's nothing compared to what I'll do to you if you become one of those monsters and threaten my family with your unnatural curse.'

"You can do this. You have to. I won't lose you."

Manning's voice filtered through a thick wall he couldn't penetrate. Agony soaked into his bones and set his skin afire, but the memories were so much worse. They always were. They'd kept him from changing over the three years after his rescue more effectively than the fear of his sister discovering that he was different, and the despair that she would reject him like everyone else had.

Only his father had held him captive and abused him at first. Chaining him to the wall and beating him with every instrument he could find on the nights of the full moon. Then another had joined in several months later, a man who had given Quinn a whole new meaning of the word pain. Quinn had kept from shifting to stay alive, yet begged for death by the time they were done with him. He'd become his own worst enemy every month, too afraid to die in the beginning but in too much pain to shift in the end.

"This is taking too long. Stop fighting!"

"'S unnatural. I'm unnatural," he mumbled. The pain was intensifying beyond what he'd experienced in the past. His spirit was clawing at him, trying to break its way through his barriers, but he couldn't let it.

Arms wrestled him to the floor and more liquid slid down his throat. He choked and tried to spit it out, but it was already spilling into his stomach, weakening his mind and blurring his senses. Without warning, a scream ripped from his chest as his spirit tore through his will, breaking and rebuilding until Quinn no longer knew where he left off and the creature began.

Then it was over. The memories of his past receded like fog under the burning radiance of the sun to be replaced by a new sensation that took him by surprise and filled him with an overwhelming sense of peace.

Chapter Seven

The pain evaporated, giving way to a deep satisfaction that seeped into his being as he felt his spirit rumble contentedly within. Or was that him? Quinn blinked open his eyes and looked up at Manning's face from an odd angle. A hand reached out to glide along his side, the feel of it so much softer than he was used to. He tilted his head, widening his eyes to take in the glossy black fur that covered his body. Only it wasn't his anymore, at least not the human form.

An inward chuckle resounded softly through his mind, the amusement of his spirit somehow diminishing his confusion and fear. *We did it?* The answering jolt of happiness was met with Manning's awed confirmation.

"You're beautiful. A black fox with a white tail. I should've known I'd always be hunting you. Let's see how fast you are."

The build of the large man shimmered in a bronze haze that seemed to encompass him, blurring limbs that altered too quickly for the eye to track. In the next instant, a huge black panther appeared and nuzzled playfully at his exposed belly. Quinn yipped and fumbled to his feet, swaying awkwardly at the disconcerting angle and use of muscles that were alien to him. But his spirit was there, lending strength and confidence along with the panther's solid frame until he was sure he could maneuver his new body on his own.

Manning nipped him on the shoulder then sped out of the open front door and into the night. Whether the instinct to join the feline belonged to him or his spirit, he wasn't sure, and neither did it matter. He ran out of the apartment as fast as he could and gave chase.

The forest was a new world waiting to be discovered and for the first few hours, it captured Quinn's fascination more than anything else. His spirit's joy was his, and they reveled in each other's delight. Then Manning showed him what it was to be hunted, and to be the hunter. Both thrilled him beyond measure, but it was the moment the feline's teeth clamped onto his ruff and he, in return, tackled the cat to the ground with canines and claws that he knew what true freedom was.

There was no fear. No pain or torn flesh. The moment was simply...natural.

And as he looked into the eyes of the fierce feline and found only endless patience, his heart soared with wonder. This might not be his forever, but it was his right now, and he wanted it more than anything.

* * * *

Manning nudged the dragging form of his mate's fox through the front door and into the living room. Quinn's energy had crashed just before sunrise, but fortunately they'd been close to the apartment. After Manning shifted swiftly, he knelt on one knee and scratched behind the fox's ears.

"Take back your human form now, pup. It's time to go to bed."

The sleek animal cocked its head to the side then shifted in a haze to reshape itself into the body of a man, but it wasn't the same body he'd seen and touched the previous night. Manning sucked in a breath at the Quinn before him. Gone were the faint protrusions of bones and the conclave belly, the evidence of a poor diet and stress, and in their place were toned, sinuous muscles that stretched the length of a taller, thicker body. Quinn was still smaller than average, finely boned and exquisitely pale, but he no longer appeared fragile.

The development of the physical body during the first change was the shifter's way of maturing just as its spirit did, and damn, it looked good on Quinn. Long overdue, but definitely worth the wait. He only wished he could be there to see the man's reaction to his new look. With a sigh, he scooped up his drowsing mate and carried him to the bedroom. Quinn was fast asleep by the time Manning pulled the covers up under his chin. As he brushed the waves of his mate's silken, loose hair back, he bent to kiss his forehead then returned to the living room to clean up. When order was restored once again, he groaned as he sat to tug his jeans on.

It'd been a long night, and it was going to be an even longer morning. He couldn't leave until he was sure that Merebeth and George were awake and that his mate was safe.

"Stay."

Manning turned at the quiet plea from the hallway. Quinn was leaning against the wall at the entrance to the living room, naked and looking utterly exhausted. Instantly, Manning tossed his pants to the side, got up and wrapped him in a hug.

"Go back to sleep. I'll be right outside."

"Please stay." Quinn stared up at him. "With me. I want you to."

Manning frowned. "Quinn—"

"I know what I'm asking. I can't be everything you need. I can't..."

"Bond with me," he supplied, reading between the lines of his mate's hesitancy. The clues had been there all along, though he'd refused to see them until only recently. At first he'd thought that it was him his mate objected to, but the time they'd spent with Cassie had revealed more than his mate likely realized. The woman had shown protective instincts toward Quinn that went well beyond friendship. Combined with Quinn's reticence to accept him as a mate and he could only conclude that the man was afraid to commit, to get hurt. And what could be more damaging than the broken promise of a sacred bond if Manning ever left him?

His mate needed time to learn the true meaning of a bond and to trust in him, time he would gladly give. The sorrow on Quinn's face wrenched at his heart.

"I'm sorry, but I need you, if it's not too late."

Funny how nearly a week ago had been too late, yet now, he'd give Quinn all the time in the world if it got him these results. "I need you too, pup." Gently lifting the man into his arms, he walked them both back to the bedroom and lay down with Quinn tucked firmly into his side. On the dresser stood the aquarium he'd bought Quinn for the turtle inside.

"So have you named our little guy yet?"

Quinn buried his face in the crook of his neck and mumbled something.

"What?"

"*Penche.*"

Old man? Manning grabbed onto Quinn's waist and dug his fingers in, tickling until cries of mercy rang out between peals of laughter. When he subsided, he closed his eyes and relaxed with the warm weight of his mate beside him.

Well, if he was old, he was still good. At least at some things.

Sometime later, the feel of smooth skin gliding across his drifted along the edge of his consciousness. Fingers quested lightly over his chest and abs and something moist dipped into the hollows just beneath his ribcage. Manning rolled onto his back and felt the sensations stop, only to resume a minute later. As he inhaled deeply, a rich aroma tinged with the smell of rain filled his lungs and permeated his being. He recognized the dream immediately as one he had every time he slept, of the man who dominated his thoughts. Only in his dreams, he was always the one doing the touching.

Something was different. Manning blinked open his eyes to find Quinn straddling one of his thighs, bent over and exploring his body with gentle hands and a roaming mouth. He made sure to keep his breathing even but didn't move, didn't make a sound for fear the man would stop if he discovered him awake. Long, black strands hid Quinn's face from view but the rest of his body was exposed, the blankets pulled back to the foot of the bed.

Manning kept his lids partially closed as Quinn moved lower to brush the thatch at his groin. Blood rushed down to the area as his mate palmed the base of his semi-erect cock and gave it a gentle squeeze. Biting his lip to keep from gasping, he watched as a small, pink tongue darted out to flick the slit on the tip of his shaft then circle lazily around the head. When his mate leaned forward and opened wide to take half of his thickening length into the scorching heat of his mouth, an involuntary hiss slipped out. Quinn jerked and looked up at him with wide eyes.

Were they…? Manning reached down and threaded his fingers through Quinn's hair to pull it back from his face. Quinn's irises were the most amazing shade of green he'd ever seen. Small flecks of yellow made them shimmer radiantly in the late afternoon light shining in from the window. Pride and overwhelming joy filled him to know he had helped to enable that change, and that the lust in them was for him.

"You're beautiful," he whispered. They stared at each other for several seconds and his stomach lurched with a flicker of apprehension, afraid Quinn might pull away. The feeling dissipated, however, when a smile spread across the man's face. Quinn dipped again and exhaled right before swallowing his stiff member all the way to the hilt. The combination of his hot breath and tight suction as he came back up drew a long groan from Manning. His mate did it over and over again, never choking or faltering in his sensuous rhythm. The feel of it was incredible, but the fact that it was Quinn spiked his desire and hardened him to the point of near pain.

Then that mouth left his straining cock and moved down to his testicles. Greedily, Quinn sucked in one of his balls and rolled it around languidly. He switched to the other and took his time bathing it and drawing it farther into the cavern of his mouth. Lower still,

Manning felt the rough surface of his mate's tongue lick along his perineum and he gasped out loud at the new sensation. No one had ever found that particular spot on him and given it attention. He widened his legs to allow for better access and fisted Quinn's hair as that tongue slid from his clenching hole to the base of his balls, heightening his arousal with each swipe.

"Fuck, where did you learn to do that?"

Quinn looked up and managed to give him a droll stare from sparkling, mischievous eyes.

"Don't answer that," Manning growled. "Just do it again." His cock twitched as his mate continued to drive him to the brink of madness. Then his cell phone went off. Quinn paused, but Manning shook his head. "Ignore it. It's in the other room and if you stop now, I think I might go insane."

His mate chuckled and was on him in the next heartbeat. Manning grunted and thrust his hips as his cock was engulfed in one swift move. Throat muscles convulsed around the head and his entire body flexed with the effort to restrain himself from throwing the man down and taking him right then.

After four rings, the phone went silent but started up again less than a minute later.

"Agh!" Manning shouted. The only people who were that persistent in reaching him were his father and his *Ketai*, and they only did so when it was urgent. Quinn shuffled to the side as he stood, but Manning picked him up and swung him over his shoulder. "Oh, no you don't. I'm not letting go of you till you finish." His mate laughed loudly then yelped as Manning smacked him on the ass smartly.

In the living room, he dug his phone from his pants pocket and answered it one-handed. "Manning."

"Where the hell are you?" Tailor yelled from the other end. "We've been waiting on you all morning."

"Tailor, do you have an emergency?"

"Umm... Not exactly, but—"

"Well I do. Unless someone's dying, don't call me again."

"Wait—"

Manning tossed the phone through the kitchen entrance then headed back to the bedroom. He threw Quinn onto the bed and jumped on top before the man had stopped bouncing.

"Was that important?" Quinn asked breathlessly.

He brought his larger body down over his mate's, groaning as his throbbing length came in contact with Quinn's own hard erection. "Nothing is as important as you." Manning started as he saw moisture glisten on his mate's thick lashes. "What is it, pup?"

Quinn shook his head and closed his eyes, then opened them again. A slow grin lifted his lips as he answered, "That was good."

Manning chuckled softly. "I try." He brought their lips together and delved in the moment Quinn parted for him. Hands began to push at his chest, but he didn't budge, satisfied to be where he was. Teeth bit down on his bottom lip, but it only caused adrenaline to rush through his system.

"Wait. Stop," Quinn panted against him. When Manning finally pulled back, the smaller man stretched over to the drawer of the nightstand and withdrew a clear bottle of liquid. Handing it to Manning, he said, "I need you in me."

Manning took the bottle of lube but frowned at his mate. "Are you sure?" As Quinn nodded vigorously, his chest began to thrum with excitement. "Hold on.

Where did you get this?" As far as he knew, Quinn never went into town by himself.

With a shy grin, Quinn answered, "Cassie gave it to me yesterday."

Score one for the woman. "Remind me to tell her I owe her one." His hands fairly shook with anticipation as he coated his fingers and cock with the liquid then placed the bottle on the nightstand. Quinn bent his legs and spread them to accommodate Manning's girth. As Manning kissed his way down his mate's neck and chest, he reached with one hand to find the man's hole. He wasn't too sure about what he was doing, but he knew the mechanics and had plenty of experience with using his fingers for pleasure.

After rubbing the puckered entrance, he pushed one finger in but stopped at the second knuckle. It was so tight. He'd tear the man apart if he tried to fit in there. "Baby, I don't think this is going to work. I don't want to hurt you."

Mentally, he went over the discussion he'd had with Tailor a few nights prior. His friend, being well versed in the acts of sex with women, men and both at once, had taken it upon himself to teach Manning, much to Manning's chagrin but for which he was now grateful. As far as he'd been told, intercourse between males was much the same as that between a man and a woman, with the exception of the importance of lube and stretching the entrance. Tailor had even commented, with a little too much enthusiasm, that it was often better. But he'd never mentioned how tiny the hole could be. To impale Quinn with his fully erect member seemed impossible without hurting him.

Quinn merely smiled up at him. "It's okay. You just need to stretch me."

"Like this?" He slid his finger all the way in then twisted it around. Inside, the tip rubbed across a soft nub of tissue and Quinn threw his head back with a gasp.

"Yeah. Right there."

Manning rubbed over that same spot again and again, adding another finger and working the tight muscle of the outer ring. By the time he added a third, Quinn was writhing beneath him, whimpering and moaning until Manning thought he might come from those sounds alone. His nervousness took a back seat to the compelling urge to push his mate to the edge, to possess all that he had to give.

"I'm ready. Please…" Quinn panted.

"Please what, baby? What do you want me to do?" He had to hear the words. Had to know his mate wanted this as much as he did.

"Please fuck me. Now!"

Manning yanked his fingers free and lifted the man's legs higher so that the head of his cock was lined up with Quinn's entrance. Slowly, he pushed in until the head was firmly inside then leaned forward to kiss his mate's swollen lips. It took every ounce of his strength to keep from plunging into Quinn's clenching depths, and inch by inch, he drove himself forward while watching his mate for signs of stress, but there were none. When he was fully encased in the hot sheath, he paused to give his mate time to adjust. It didn't take long.

"Move. You have to move."

Manning began easing himself in and out, burying his cock as far as it could go with each deep thrust. He delved again into Quinn's mouth and became lost in the heady feel of heat and muscles gripping him mercilessly. This was beyond anything he'd ever imagined sex could be and so much more than the physical act. Knowing Quinn trusted him enough to do this brought out emotions he'd never felt before. It was humbling and exhilarating at the same time.

Soon, his body was taking over. He quickened his pace and plunged deeper, thrilling in the way Quinn met each one of his hard thrusts.

"Harder. Oh, fuck," Quinn moaned.

Unable to hold back any longer, he sat up, grabbed his mate's thighs and slammed himself in. He set up a brutal rhythm that he was sure would split the smaller man in two, but the sheer pleasure rolling off Quinn in waves spurred him on. The sudden compulsion to claim his mate threatened to steal his control as his canines descended, but he bit into his bottom lip at the last second.

Fire raced down his spine and he felt his balls tighten with his imminent climax. Quinn arched his back and screamed, thick ropes of cum spurting from his cock and painting his sweat-slicked chest. The walls of his channel gripped Manning's cock mercilessly and sent him over the edge. He tipped his head back and roared as his orgasm blasted through him with unbelievable force. Tremors shook his body as he shot his seed deep into his mate's strangling sheath.

When the storm of pleasure finally passed and he was able to move again, he released Quinn's thighs then immediately cursed. Four dark bruises marked each of his mate's legs from the crushing grip of his fingers. Panic rushed in and he looked down to find Quinn staring sleepily up at him.

He brushed the damp hair from his mate's forehead and said, "I'm sorry. I promised I wouldn't hurt you."

Quinn merely pulled him down into a tight embrace. "You didn't hurt me. I loved it. That was amazing."

Manning smiled and allowed himself to relax into his mate's hold. Damn, this was worth everything. The slide of a tongue across the pulsing vein in his neck made him shiver. He felt the scrape of a sharp, a very sharp canine, along his skin and was about to lean into it instinctively when Quinn jerked back.

A hand flew to his mate's mouth and through it he mumbled, "I have to go."

"Where?"

"To see Cassie." Quinn moved his hand to explain, "She's leaving tomorrow morning and I promised to visit her before then."

Manning frowned as he slid from his mate and moved to stand, confused by the hint of alarm in his mate's tone. "We still have the rest of the day. Let's take a shower then head over there."

"No. You don't have to—"

"Quinn, whether we bond or not, you will always be my mate. I can't let you go anywhere without protection until I get a few matters settled."

Quinn's brows drew down. "You don't care if we never bond?"

Is that what he'd said? Damn, there was just no good way to answer that. This could be a case of open mouth, insert foot or... No, that about summed it up.

Manning decided to go with the truth and pray he wasn't restricted to watching over his mate from the outdoors again. "Three weeks ago, I thought I'd never see you again. Three days ago, I was afraid that I could never earn your trust and this morning, I was afraid I wouldn't be here to see your reaction to your new body."

"My new... What?"

"Never mind. My point is, I want a family and a home and, eventually, love. I can't see that happening with anyone but you, and I think since we've gotten this far, we can make it the rest of the way. None of that requires us to be bonded. I just want...this." He waved his hand to indicate the both of them, breathing a sigh of relief when Quinn smiled.

"I'll start the shower." He got up to go to the bathroom while Manning finished making the bed. "Oh shit!" Back in the bedroom, he skidded to a halt and stared at Manning wide-eyed. "How?"

Manning grinned at his mate's flushed excitement. "It's the shifters' way of maturing with their spirit. It's also why the first change is the hardest. Tonight will go a lot smoother."

Quinn glanced from the dresser mirror back to him then grinned. "I look good."

Manning laughed and kissed his mate before turning him around and smacking him on the ass. "You've always looked good, now go start the shower. I'll be there in a sec."

After they showered, Manning went alone to his house to change clothes as Quinn had insisted on staying behind to wait for him. He didn't understand his mate's reluctance to venture out into the rest of the community but didn't want to pry. In town, he treated Quinn and Cassie to dinner and a movie. The little human was overflowing with enthusiasm over Quinn's sudden physical development but, oddly, didn't ask a single question about it. From the amount of times she winked conspiratorially at Quinn and his mate's subsequent blushes, it was obvious she'd guessed what had gone on since the last time she'd seen them.

At the end of the evening, she again requested to be alone with Quinn in her hotel room. When his mate came back out, Cassie's floral scent clung to him strongly, as it had the previous night, but Manning didn't comment. Though he had to admit that if he weren't absolutely sure his mate was gay, he would've been jealous. They made it back to the apartment in time for Manning to coach Quinn about shifting with his clothes on. This required a little more concentration, but his mate pulled it off beautifully.

They ran through dense forestry under the cloak of night for several hours and, although their communication was restricted, Quinn picked up on his cues easily and felled his first prey. After that, it was hard to keep the fox's excitement in check, but Manning didn't mind. The thrill of seeing his mate come alive and learn to love the gift the Mother had bequeathed to them was like reliving his own first change. When the temperature rose a few degrees, heralding the coming of dawn, he noticed they were closer to his house than Merebeth's and decided to take his mate there.

As they broke through the line of trees and came into view of the small mansion, Quinn backed away into the shadows of the thick brush. When Manning tried to urge him to follow, he only shied away farther. Manning shifted to his human form then crouched down so that he was at eyelevel with the fox. In his spirit's form, Quinn was more prone to instinct than logical reasoning.

"This is my house. I promise you it's safe, and we can travel back to your apartment after we've rested." The fox stared unblinkingly for so long, he was about to repeat his assurance but stopped when its shape blurred and Quinn took its place.

"Are there others here?"

"Only my father. The others always take this time of the month to run and visit with family and friends. They won't be back until tomorrow night."

His mate stepped hesitantly onto the cultivated lawn and crossed the distance between them. "So... Is your father's room close to yours?"

"Not really. Why?"

Quinn rubbed his body seductively along the front of Manning's and whispered in his ear, "Because I want to do bad things to you."

Manning's cock hardened so fast it took his brain a few moments to catch up. With a growl, he lifted his mate by the ass, their erections coming together as Quinn circled his legs around Manning's waist. He didn't remember carrying his mate to the front door or walking the expanse of the living room and corridor to his room on the far left side of the house. Quinn's kisses, his drugging scent and soft whimpers, made everything else disappear as if they existed in a world apart from reality. Manning felt disconnected from the demands of his position and the personal responsibility of revenge.

With Quinn, he found solace, and with or without a bond, this connection was what he wanted.

Chapter Eight

The sun was up and blazing in the sky by the time he roused himself from sleep. Manning squinted against the bright rays pouring in from his bedroom window and tried to turn to shelter his eyes but was unsuccessful. A glance down revealed Quinn's body draped completely over his with legs bent on either side of his waist, arms crossed around the back of his neck and face buried just beneath his chin. There was no possible way to move the man without waking him, but Manning wasn't sure he wanted to.

The tingling call of nature, however, had other plans for him.

Manning gently rolled his mate over and chuckled as Quinn strengthened his hold and groaned plaintively. "Time to get up, pup."

"I don't want to," Quinn murmured against his skin.

"Come on. While we're here, I want you to meet my father." Gray eyes popped open as Quinn reared back to stare at him. "Now that I have you, he won't be here for long. I want you to know him before he goes."

"I forgot about that custom. Of course."

When Quinn continued to hold him with a searching gaze, he smiled sadly. "It's okay. I've had a lot of time to deal with the knowledge that he'll follow my mom. He'd have done it sooner, but it took me a while to find you."

"Does he know I'm a guy?"

"Yes. Among shifters, it doesn't matter, especially when it comes to mates."

Quinn shaded his eyes and slipped from the bed.

"Quinn?"

"Will you take a shower with me?"

Something was bothering his mate, but he didn't want to press the issue. "Sure." After they showered and dressed in only pants and shirts, they came across his father walking to the kitchen. The older man smiled hugely when he saw them coming.

"Dad, this is Quinn. Quinn, my father."

Quinn extended his hand when they were close enough. "Mr Stone."

Adan took the hand and pulled Quinn into a hug, laughing as if he couldn't contain himself. "That's Dad to you, son." He pushed Quinn back to arm's length and said, "Damn, you look good. Thought I'd never see the day. Manning is one lucky man. Come on, I was just about to make lunch. You like steak, right? Of course you do. I'll make yours rare."

Quinn sent Manning a panicked expression as Adan led him to the kitchen, and he sent back a shrug. He'd known his father would be excited but even he hadn't expected that much of a reaction. In the kitchen, he headed for the coffee pot on the other side but paused at the slight tremor in his mate's voice.

"Mr Stone..."

"Dad."

"Umm… I'm sorry, but I think I should go. I'm late for work."

Manning was about to object when his father raised a hand to silence him. "Manning, can you go out to the garage and get those deer steaks we have in the freezer?"

If it were anyone but his father, he'd have said no on the spot, but he knew Quinn would be safe with Adan. "I'll be right back," he said, kissing his mate and offering a smile of encouragement.

He left before Quinn could protest. From the chest freezer in the garage, he pulled out three frozen steaks then made his way again across the extensive mansion. By the time he arrived back at the kitchen, much to his surprise, Quinn was sitting at the table with his father and laughing without an ounce of uneasiness.

"Okay, what did I miss?"

Adan stood and took the steaks from him. "I was just telling your mate about your first shift. How you were too impatient to pay attention to my lessons and couldn't tell the difference between a mound of dead leaves and a pile of bear crap."

Manning scowled as Quinn quirked a brow at him.

"Head first, huh?"

"Slipped right in the shit and fell head first into a stream." Adan chuckled. "We couldn't get him near a body of water for a year after that."

"Thanks, Dad," he said dryly. At least his father hadn't mentioned the time—

"Don't worry. I'll tell him about the time you mistook Brack for a female in his tiger form the next time you leave the room."

Wonderful. Now his day was complete, but he couldn't help but grin when Quinn laughed again.

That sound was worth reliving his humiliation. When the steaks were defrosted and they were ready to move out to the verandah to put them on the barbeque pit, Manning excused himself and went to his study upstairs. After closing the door, he went to the window to watch Quinn and his father while he dialed the Alpha of the community on his cell phone.

"Manning?" Armand's voice was gruff and hollow.

"Rough night?"

"And humans think they have it bad. At least when their kids turn eighteen, they can kick them out of the house. How the hell am I supposed to teach my kid to fly when I'm a boar?"

Manning gave a light chuckle. He'd forgotten the Alpha's kids were due to mature this year. "Don't you have twins?"

"Don't get me started."

"I'll send Tailor over to give him a few pointers. Listen, I was wondering if you and your Betas could come over in a few hours to welcome my mate to the community. I know newcomers are generally supposed to meet the entire pack, but he's a little gun shy and I want to ease him into becoming a member."

"No problem. I'll call my men and see you soon."

"Thanks, Armand." He hung up and looked out on his mate and father. He didn't like setting up a meeting without Quinn's knowledge but had a feeling it was the only way to get the man to come out of his shell. Quinn needed to learn he was welcome within the community. Being accepted would boost his confidence and help to ease his nervousness around others. Manning had noticed his mate's reaction to the crowds in town and was sure Quinn would find it easier to socialize with his own kind.

Back downstairs, he joined them at the outdoor table and took the plate of food his father handed him. The conversation remained light until Adan surprised him again by talking about his mother. Her name hadn't passed the man's lips since she'd been gone, but he spoke of her fondly to Quinn, bringing her back to life through memories so Quinn could know the warm soul who would have loved him.

Eventually, his father stood and cleared his throat. "Well, I need to get in and finish up that paperwork Manning's been putting off."

Manning winced at the reminder of the duties his father had temporarily taken over for him. "I can take care of it once I drop Quinn off in a few."

Adan shook his head and waved a hand. "Don't worry about it. I was *Jaes'din* for more than sixty years. I know what I'm doing. Take more time with your mate. He's worth it," the man said with a wink to Quinn. "I'll be in the study if you need me."

When they were alone, Manning gathered the dishes and took them to the sink in the kitchen. Two arms wrapped around him from behind and he turned around to see his mate smiling up at him.

"I like your dad. I'm sure I would've liked your mom too."

"He's right, you know. She would have loved everything about you."

Quinn hugged him tighter, kissing his neck. "I'm sorry I didn't get to meet her."

Manning squeezed back, inhaling deeply of the man's intoxicating scent. Everything about his mate called to him. Quinn's smell, his compassion and the way his body fit so perfectly against his. He found it hard to imagine a bond could make him feel any more complete than he already did.

He clasped Quinn's waist, spun around and lifted him onto the counter. The sound of his mate's gasp was swallowed as he brought their mouths together in a heated kiss. A wave of desire blended with one of his own and he crushed Quinn to him, reveling in the arousal he ignited within his mate. Quinn's tongue met his stroke for stroke, his fingers sliding underneath the hem of his shirt.

Manning knew he would never get enough of this. The way Quinn's body responded and came alive at his touch, the way he not only succumbed to passion, but sought after it now with an urgency Manning could feel with all of his senses, was heady and thrilling. Gone was the timid lover hiding in a shell of safety and in his place was a man unafraid to show Manning what he wanted, as he'd proven last night. Several times. His mate had been insatiable and the memory of it had his cock straining against the seam of his pants as though months had passed since it had last been granted release.

Manning broke away only long enough to tug Quinn's shirt over his head then dove back, seeking out every moist crevice of his mate's mouth.

"What are you doing?" Quinn whispered around the press of lips locked to his.

"Making up for lost time." Without pulling back, he unfastened his mate's jeans and tightly grasped the hard erection that popped free. Quinn shuddered with a soft whimper as Manning pumped him a few times then rubbed his thumb across the weeping slit, spreading the evidence of his arousal around the flared head. "Two weeks you made me chase after you when you were here the whole time. I figure you still owe me."

Quinn chuckled then arched back with a breathless cry as Manning began pumping again, squeezing his long cock from base to tip. "What…? What about your dad?"

Manning dipped his head to suck strongly on the curve of his mate's neck, inhaling deeply of the wild aroma drenching his senses. "He's upstairs in the study. Won't hear a thing." The flesh beneath his lips vibrated with a low moan. Quinn's energy and movements became more insistent, his nails raking lightly up the sides of Manning's ribs before his fingers clutched the base of Manning's skull and urged it down for another kiss.

"Fuck me, please. I want you inside me when I come."

Manning growled at the desperate plea and fumbled with his pants as Quinn jumped off the counter to strip out of his jeans. He almost felt like a virgin getting his first taste of forbidden ecstasy. Not because he was nervous, but because he knew how much it cost his mate to give in to desire and trust that there was nothing to fear. The knowledge that he was Quinn's first lover since his teen years was humbling and filled him with honor at the same time.

"Shit, I forgot the lube in the bedroom."

Quinn gave a lopsided grin then stepped close, lifting one of Manning's hands and drawing two fingers into the damp heat of his mouth. Manning's eyes rolled back, his cock jerking at the sensation of his mate's tongue swirling and slicking the entire length of his fingers. When he could focus again, it was the sight of Quinn's half-lidded eyes changing from gray to molten green that snapped the rest of his patience.

Unable to hold back any longer, he grabbed Quinn by the waist and lifted him until his mate's legs were wrapped firmly around him. Their mouths came together furiously now as Manning walked them to the nearest bare wall, shoving Quinn against it while driving his moistened fingers into his mate's clenching entrance. Another growl came out as he found it still loose from the night before. Even so, he stretched the sensitive ring as much as he could from the odd angle, feeling as though he might burst from the whimpering pants his mate was emitting.

"Now. Please, now."

Manning extracted his fingers, lined up the tip of his pulsing cock with Quinn's hole, and plunged in. Quinn shifted his pelvis, using the weight of his body to drive himself farther down until Manning's shaft was completely engulfed in scorching heat. The incredible feel of muscles contracting around him, the increased volume of his mate's gasping cries and the stimulating scent of his lust all came to be too much. It was only by sheer will that he kept his canines from dropping, but he couldn't restrain the overpowering need to command the body riding his, to make it yield to his desire and take all that he had to give.

After he took hold of Quinn's hips, he thrust with unrelenting intent, pounding as deep as he could go into his mate's gripping depths. Quinn clasped onto his shoulders as he leaned back and Manning knew he was hitting the man's prostate when Quinn rolled his head from side to side, nails digging into skin. Fire raced through his blood as undeniable pressure built in his groin. He could feel his orgasm building like a tidal wave surging through his veins.

Quinn met each of his hard lunges with an eagerness that drove him to the verge of frenzy. When his mate's back stiffened and he leaned forward to bury his face in the crook of Manning's neck, he knew Quinn was almost there.

"Come for me, baby. Come all over me."

Quinn let out a strangled cry just before heat splashed between them, the walls of his channel clamping down mercilessly onto Manning's driving member, but it was the feel of two sharp canines dragging along the hollow of his neck that pushed him over the edge. His own canines ruptured from his gums as his cock exploded with an orgasm that took his breath away. The driving release consumed his body and stole his thoughts until nothing else existed. Only Quinn and the warmth of his surrounding embrace, the solace of his pleasure.

Manning trembled once, twice, as Quinn ran his tongue seductively over the place where his teeth had grazed. He struggled to regain his equilibrium and gently lifted his mate to lower him to the floor. "I think we're going to need a lot more showers before the day is over."

Quinn tipped his head back and laughed. "Maybe, but I really should head back. I don't want Merebeth to get worried."

He gave a nod and one last, lingering kiss before releasing him to find their pants. They still had the kitchen to clean, which should take just long enough for the Alpha and his Betas to arrive. Clothed again, Quinn joined him at the sink, but they both paused as a loud crash came from beyond the kitchen door. Another crash, seconds later and closer this time, was followed by myriad angry shouts and animalistic growls.

His father's voice rose above the noise, yelling, "Manning, stop them!"

Alarm shot through him and he ordered Quinn to stay where he was then ran to the door only to skid to a halt as one of Armand's Betas burst into the room. With claws unsheathed and feral eyes flashing, the large man snarled in rage, but Manning could swear it was lust he scented on the Beta. Another of Armand's Betas tore the kitchen door from its hinges while a third came rushing in after him, both in the same wild state as the first and both reeking of lust and rage.

In the next moment, a hiss sounded from behind Manning and he turned back to his mate. Quinn was crouched in a fighting stance, irises black but for a thin, outer ring of dark red and fangs extended nearly an inch past the row of his top teeth.

Fangs. Not canines.

Shock and anger coursed through him, but the sight was lost in the next instant. The first Beta grabbed onto Manning's neck and threw him across the room where he crashed into the wall then fell to the floor. A fourth Beta rushed past him and he jumped up in time to kick him in the chest, sending him flying back into a confused Armand. Manning ran to the third and shoved the man hard into the counter of the island, bashing his head onto the tiled surface.

From the corner of his eye, he saw Quinn punch the first Beta and jam his knee into the gut of the second. The fourth leaped past Manning and came up behind Quinn, who brought his elbow back in a vicious jab to the man's nose, but he wasn't in time to stop the next attack of the first. The man sank his teeth deep into the crevice of Quinn's neck and the subsequent scream racked Manning with chills. All three men tackled his mate to the ground then, ripping off his clothes and tearing into his skin with their claws and canines.

Manning surged forward and snatched at the nearest man. His mate's blood-covered body caught his attention as he tossed the man to the side, and blinding fury suffused his entire being. "Enough!" he shouted.

Everyone froze under the power of the *Jaes'din's* voice, but when he looked back to Quinn, he found only the two Betas on the floor. Manning tracked a thick trail of blood from the floor to the counter and beyond the frame of the shattered window above it. *Vam'kir* were gifted with speed, but he'd had no idea they were that fast.

Manning felt his world spiral with uncontrollable turbulence as shock gave way to a fury of emotions. Quinn was *Vam'kir*, and Quinn was gone.

* * * *

Pain lived in every fiber of his being, burning through his skin and muscles until his bones shook with the effort to carry him in his flight, but that wasn't what slowed him down. Streams of tears clouded his vision and caused him to trip over every tree root and small bush in his path.

The anger and horror on Manning's face as he'd realized what Quinn was seared his heart like a branding iron. How could he have been so stupid? He'd known the risk of staying at Manning's house, yet he'd ignored it in favor of his fucking hormones. Hormones he knew might have a chance of setting off unmated shifters just as they did trancers, and now his mate had seen the damning evidence of his true nature, and his curse.

Quinn stumbled over a fallen tree and hit the ground, his strength fading fast, but he pushed to his feet in stubborn determination. The slatted rooftop of Merebeth's cottage came into view about a quarter mile ahead. Just a little farther. It was imperative he pack his things and leave before Manning got there.

He couldn't bear to see the hatred on his mate's face when he came to demand answers, or even worse, send him back to France and into the hands of his tormentor. Quinn would rather die before that happened.

As he limped into the front yard, George came around the other side of the cottage carrying a tool case. The man dropped it the moment their eyes met and rushed forward.

"Shit! Merebeth!"

Quinn tried to push him away but George easily overpowered him and swept him up into large arms. "Let go of me."

"Merebeth!"

Merebeth came running out of the front door, nearly falling on the steps when she saw Quinn.

"Sweet Mother of Creation! What happened?"

"You know what happened," George ground out as he carried Quinn into the living room and laid him on the couch. "Take care of him. I'm going to kill that bastard."

Quinn tried to struggle against the couple's hands pushing him down but was too weak from blood loss. "Let me up."

"George—" Merebeth started.

"I told him. *You* told him not to bring Quinn around other shifters until he was ready."

"I was going to tell you to take care of Quinn yourself. I'm the only one who can stop Manning. I'm going to tan that boy's hide and make him wish for death."

"No!" Quinn shouted. "It's not his fault. There's something wrong with me."

Merebeth came around to his front and clamped one hand onto the wound on his neck, using the other to remove the tatters of his shirt. "Sweetie, you're the *Aucinthe*. You haven't gotten that far in the book yet, but there is nothing wrong with you. Manning was careless and ignored our warnings."

"Beth, he's losing too much blood. We need to get him a donor," George said, assessing the injuries on his arms and chest.

"I know of a human. Get my phone."

Just then, the furious roar of a feline came from the open front door and Quinn craned his neck to see the form of Manning's panther bounding into the room. George blurred instantly and took on the shape of a huge lion that must have outweighed the panther by at least a hundred pounds. Quinn used the last of his strength to push Merebeth's hands away and jump up from the couch.

"Stop!"

The two animals collided with a resounding crash and attacked each other in a flurry of claws and teeth.

"Stop!" Merebeth repeated, but this time the animals obeyed.

Quinn dropped to the floor, fading into unconsciousness.

Chapter Nine

Soft whispers grated along his nerves, dragging him from the peaceful depths of sleep. He fought against the disturbance but it clutched at his consciousness and refused to let go. Eventually, the whispers ceased behind the quiet click of a door. Unable to descend back into oblivion, he reached out with his senses to get a feel for his surroundings. The air was warm, with a mild breeze blowing across his face. There was silence but for the melodic trilling of birds at a distance and a low, rumbling snore toward his feet.

Merebeth's sugary sweet fragrance permeated the air, along with George's woodland spice. An undercurrent of bacon and eggs made his stomach pang with hunger, but it was the last smell he recognized that sent a shiver down his spine. The familiar scents of pine and musk seeped into his pores with such subdued vitality, it was nearly nonexistent. He was almost afraid to exhale for fear the scents might be blown away.

Quinn opened his eyes and squinted against the bright rays of sunlight cascading in from an open window on his right. With more energy than he cared to admit was necessary, he pulled one hand from the blanket that covered him and swiped at the reactive tears in his eyes. His first look around revealed a collage of Merebeth's personal effects and decorations, which seemed to fall into a sort of ordered chaos that somehow created the feel of intimate comfort.

A weight prevented him from moving his legs and he looked down to find Manning draped over them. The man was sitting in a chair pulled up to the side of the bed with his chest on Quinn's shins and his head resting on folded arms. Stubble covered his jaw and deep creases lined his forehead and the corners of his mouth. If shifters aged in human years, Quinn would think the man was bordering his late fifties.

A lock of hair tickled Quinn's cheek and the tug of his muscles as he moved to strip it back caused him to hiss. Damn, it had been a while since he'd felt that kind of pain. No doubt the skin around his wounds had sealed, but the muscles always took longer to mend.

Manning shot up with a start, eyes alert though bloodshot and rimmed with soreness. His short black hair was spiked in every direction and furrows on one side of his face from the blanket added to his haggard appearance. Quinn held his breath, at a loss as to what to expect.

"Hi," Manning said in a gruff voice.

Quinn blinked, cleared his throat then replied, "Hi."

Slowly, Manning reached over to the nightstand and picked up a glass of water with a straw in it. Quinn lifted his head to drink deeply then gasped as the man moved to set it down. Four long scars ran parallel to each other down Manning's forearm. They could only be the remnants of his clash with George, which brought the memory of the incident back to Quinn's mind with jarring clarity.

"George."

"He's fine," Manning provided. "A few scratches and Merebeth's been pampering him like a king."

"You shouldn't have attacked him to get to me."

The man creased his forehead in confusion. "You're my mate and you were hurt. I'd go through anyone to get to you."

Manning's response seemed to stem from such a different context that it threw Quinn off. "You don't want to send me back to France or...kill me?"

Manning flinched as though struck then sat back and stared at him for several long seconds. "Is that why you thought I was after you?"

Quinn wondered briefly if George hadn't caused a little damage in the brain area during their scrap. "I am *Vam'kir.*"

The chair toppled back as Manning stood abruptly. He gripped his head with both hands and began to pace in brisk strides then stopped to fix Quinn with a hard stare. "You are my mate. Tell me. Tell me what happened in your past that makes you think you're so unworthy of being cared for, of being loved. Help me understand so that I stop making so many mistakes when it comes to you."

Tears formed, but he blinked them back. He would not let the man change the subject. "I saw the look on your face when you realized what I was," Quinn seethed, fine tremors shaking his voice. "You hated me."

"I was angry because you lied to me, but I can't blame you for that. I could never hate you."

"My kind killed your mother."

"Members of the *Vam'kir* killed my mother," Manning said just as vehemently. Then, his flash of irritation seemed to dissipate with a sigh. "Tell me it's okay to condemn you for your race and I will."

Quinn gazed in stunned silence, utterly taken aback. Is that what he was doing? Trying to convince the man to hate him because of his race? Somewhere along the line, the tables had turned, but the concept that Manning could feel for him what he hadn't even dared to hope for was still too much.

"You saw what those men did to me. I'll never be normal. Every time I get aroused, every unmated shifter near me will lose control, even your friends."

"There's a reason for that, for everything, but that's not a reason why we shouldn't be together." Manning crossed to the bed and combed his fingers lightly through Quinn's hair. "If you'll give me another chance, I swear I won't fail you again."

Quinn frowned. Nothing was as it should be. This wasn't the disparaging reality he'd come to expect from life. Manning should be cursing him for his betrayal and he should be packing his things to escape persecution. Yet here he was, being asked to give forgiveness by the one person he'd been sure would've condemned him for the truth of his origins and for the madness he caused in others. This bewildering scenario was too much. He needed time to process what was going on.

"I need to go to the bathroom." When Manning nodded and reached to help him from the bed, he shook his head. "I can make it." He couldn't think with the man touching him. Manning's very presence had his emotions bouncing all over the place.

Manning paused before backing away. "Merebeth will want to talk to you when you're done."

As soon as he was gone, Quinn locked his jaw and suppressed a groan as he pushed himself to a seated position. After a minute to brace himself against a wave of dizziness, he rose shakily to his feet and walked out of the room. In the bathroom at the end of the hallway, he glanced at his reflection in the mirror.

Skin too pale contrasted sharply with the dark circles under his eyes and mussed, black hair. White cotton bandages dotted his bare chest, a few colored with residual blood in their centers. Gingerly, he traced the puckered grooves of claw marks along his ribs and hips, disappearing under the band of the sweatpants he wore. A shudder racked him at the thought of what might have happened had Manning not used the power of his voice to halt the actions of those men.

He started with the bandage on the curve of his neck, peeling away the tape affixing it to his skin and inspecting the puffy ridges forming two half-moons in the shape of a bite. From the state of repair, he estimated that he'd probably been asleep for a few days. Another twenty-four hours and the evidence of the attack would be no more than a memory to add to his growing collection.

Once he'd transferred all the dressings from his body to the wastebasket, he took a shower then dressed in the same baggy sweats he'd been wearing. Merebeth was waiting for him at the doorway to her bedroom and he preceded her in at her gesture and took a seat on the side of the bed. Merebeth sat across from him in the chair she'd righted on the floor and Quinn watched her set the book she was holding in her lap. The same one she'd given him to read upon his arrival at her house.

"I was hoping you would have the time to come to this on your own, but I can see that's no longer an option."

He swallowed down the lump of rising anxiety and tracked her fingers as they flipped past the middle pages of the book, but at the same time, patience wasn't a virtue he could claim at that moment. Whatever the woman had to say undoubtedly involved the rest of the answers she'd promised him, but he was too busy struggling with other concerns. The issues of where he was going to sleep that night now that other shifters in the community were aware of his presence and what he was going to do about his current predicament with Manning rode heavily on his mind.

"Ah, here we go." She turned the book and pressed it into his hands. "This section of the book marks the birth of *Miel se Luuda's* next greatest creation, the war and sequent separation that brought about the rise of two individual races and the hope she gave us that we might one day restore what was broken."

A glance down showed script written in a mixture of *Ba'Kal* and *Vam'kir* as most of the text was, requiring the reader to be fluent in both languages to understand it, which he wasn't quite yet. "Merebeth, I don't have time for a history lesson," he said, handing the book back. "I have more important things to do."

Gentle eyes bored into him with a chastising stare that sent chills over his flesh. The same look had marked his mother's features many times when he'd misbehaved before his sexuality had driven a wedge between them. That wedge, it seemed now, had only been preparation for the severance of their relationship upon the discovery of his spirit.

"Sorry," he said.

"As the historian of the *Ba'Kal*, it is my duty to provide you with this book so that you may read the information and know it is the truth, but I suppose under the circumstances, I can make this one exception. That is if you trust that what I tell you is without my own personal influence."

Quinn was about to comment that of course he trusted her, but the solemnity in the woman's countenance stopped him. Instead, he merely nodded.

"All right, then." She ran one finger over several paragraphs, tapped it against her lips then looked back at him. "Nearly two millennia ago, the Mother of Creation gazed out in contemplation on the humans that inhabited the earth, her lands and seas, and decided to create a sentient race born of her loins called the *Bassen'kir*, or simply *Kir*. They were given special gifts that would enable them to thrive in a dangerous world.

"Each *Kir* contained the abilities of prodigious strength and speed. They were born with a spirit that, upon maturation, would meld with their souls and allow them to take on the form of their particular spirit. Her only stipulation was that they commune with her on the full moon of every month by shifting into the form of their spirits at night and drinking of the sustenance she provided during the day. The *Kir* learned to hunt the animals of the forests mostly during those two days out of the month. They would put the beasts into a trance to ease the giving of blood then store the meat to feed their communities until the next full moon."

"Wait," Quinn interrupted. "Are you saying that *Ba'Kal* and *Vam'kir* were once this single race? This...*Bassen'kir*?"

Merebeth fixed him with another stare that told him the story was only going to come out on her terms. "As I was saying, the *Kir* lived in peace with nature and even the ignorant humans, for the most part. Their numbers multiplied and, because of their significant longevity, the decision was made to branch out into other parts of the world. There were two sons born to the royal house at that time. One chose to stay in this country while the other led the group of *Kir* willing to venture overseas to the land that is now known as France.

"The son overseas began taking his sustenance from humans and, after finding it much to his liking, started instructing the others to do so as well. This created great conflict between the brothers and eventually resulted in a war that not only divided the loyalties of the *Kir*, but that also brought them to the brink of extinction. One son abandoned the act of drinking blood completely and demanded his followers do the same, while the other discarded the gift of his spirit and insisted the *Kir* who supported him do likewise."

Merebeth took a deep breath then continued. "*Miel se Luuda* was forced to alter her stipulation in order to ensure the survival of her creation. To the *Kir* who'd gone overseas and to the son who'd appointed himself their *Magnique*, their king, she granted strength, speed and life through the ingestion of blood. To the *Kir* who'd remained in this country and to the son who took on the title of their *Jaes'din*, she granted life and strength through the exchange of their forms for the spirits that resided within them. And so, two separate races came into being. The *Ba'Kal* and the *Vam'kir*.

"Each century thereafter, she created one being with all the qualities of the *Kir*. To this *Aucinthe*, she bequeathed a power that could be used to unite both races and restore them to their original glory as the *Bassen'kir*. This power, however, would remain dormant within the *Aucinthe* until he or she mated.

"Unlike the rest of us, the *Aucinthe* was given the control to bond with whomever they deemed worthy of using the power wisely, for once the bond was forged, the power would spread to whichever race the *Aucinthe's* mate belonged to. It could be used to incite another war, in which case the scales would be decidedly tipped and the race of the *Aucinthe's* mate would surely win, or it could fulfill its original purpose and be used to force the other race to admit to the kindredship between the *Ba'Kal* and *Vam'kir*."

Dread knotted Quinn's belly and it became increasingly difficult to fill his lungs with air. Merebeth was peering at him now with an expression that dared him to believe in a waking nightmare.

"I am the *Aucinthe*," he whispered.

The older woman nodded slowly. "You were created in the exact image of the *Bassen'kir* and placed in your mother's womb. The power you contain can only be detected by those of both races who are unmated. They are unwittingly driven to seek out your approval whenever they scent your interest."

"My interest? You mean my hormones?" Quinn gave a sarcastic laugh, at once overcome with anger. "Bullshit!" he hissed. "They attack me and try to force me to submit. They—" The constriction of his throat choked off the rest of his sentence.

Merebeth's eyes softened with sympathy. "The lure of the power is oft times too great for them to retain control over how they approach you. Many *Aucinthe* have died that way, while others were killed by the ruling houses of each race for fear of the loss of dominion the rulers have over their respective races.

Though the book doesn't state it, I suspect *Miel se Luuda* knows this each time she creates an *Aucinthe,* but if she were to dampen the power, it would not be enough to bring the races together."

His mind was whirling with the aspects of his life that had made no sense up until this point. The suffering and loneliness he'd endured had all been part of a divine plan that had made his life a living hell. "What will the power do?"

Merebeth frowned. "No one knows quite what it will bring about."

"Does Manning know about this?"

"He does now. Only the ruling *Magnique* and *Jaes'din* are privy to this information upon their ascension. Every hundred years when the roles are passed on to the next generation in both houses, the historian of each race is charged with providing them with the information they need to rule over their people having full knowledge of the past and the consequences of implementing a war that might annihilate the other race. For if one kind were to succeed, there's no telling what *Miel se Luuda* would do from there.

"Adan wanted to wait until his son was mated in the hopes that bonding would temper some of Manning's anger at the murder of his mother and forestall another war, then I met you, and I knew it was more important to provide you with the information first so that you could learn and decide which side to align yourself with. Though Manning is your mate, the power can be given freely to anyone you choose and trust. I've notified Xenessa, the historian of the *Vam'kir* and a good friend of mine, that you're here and she asked me to convey her regrets on failing to find you while you were among her kind. She was also wondering which clan you hailed from—"

"He knew," Quinn whispered.

Merebeth paused with a slight frown. "No dear. I promise you Manning didn't realize what you are. He would never have knowingly put you in danger..."

But Quinn's mind was no longer on the conversation, or even in the room. It was back in the cold, dark recesses of the underground prison tunnels running the length of the *Magnique's* fortress. Quinn shivered involuntarily at the memory of the dank, lightless cell into which his father had thrown him after rescuing him from the mob of crazed *Vam'kir* on the grounds of his high school. The cells hadn't been used to house *Ba'Kal* captives since the last war. The matted straw that'd covered the hard-packed dirt had been molded and teeming with fleas and other vermin, originally put there to remind the *Ba'Kal* prisoners of the beasts they were.

He'd thought the attack had led to his father's discovery of the spirit that resided within him, and that that had been the reason for the cruel punishments inflicted on him—the week and a half of starvation, the nightly beatings that would last for hours on end and the excruciating agony of being denied blood when the full moon had risen during that period of time.

Usually, the symptoms associated with blood deprivation were restricted to an intense burning sensation in the veins and along the skin. He knew now the racking pain that had infused his very bones had heralded what should have been his first transformation, which would've allowed him to mature along with his spirit.

"Quinn?" Merebeth called as though from a faraway distance.

Quinn's body began to tremble as realization set in. His father had known then that he was the *Aucinthe*. The torture had simply been a way of filling the time while his father was deciding whether to kill him, just as the introduction of Quinn's tormentor hadn't been about punishing him for being gay.

All those years of enduring his tormentor's brutal touch and fighting to keep his sanity while the man used everything at his disposal to rip away Quinn's pride and will. The vicious taking of his body and blood over and over again in an effort to force him to mate with his tormentor. That hadn't been about teaching him a lesson for daring to be a son of the *Magnique* and gay. It had all been a part of his father's design to gain the advantage over their enemy.

Had Quinn submitted... Had he given in to the futility and despair of his life and mated with his tormentor, unintentionally releasing his power, his father could have wiped out the entire race of *Ba'Kal.*

He would have been responsible for the decimation of one half of the Mother's greatest creation. The power he contained was...

Quinn jumped up from the bed, ran back to the bathroom and lifted the toilet seat. Bile spewed forth the moment his knees hit the tiled floor and sweat drenched every inch of his skin by the time his stomach ceased its violent spasms. A cold, wet rag was pressed to his temple and he took it gratefully, but when he looked up into Merebeth's tender expression, slivers of ice pierced his flesh.

I could have killed her.

The knowledge ricocheted inside his mind until it was all he could do not to scream out his guilt. At the end of his four-year imprisonment, his life had become unbearable and he'd been ready to give in to the demands of his tormentor. He would have, had Mara not found him at that moment and taken the choice from him. If his tormentor caught him now, he wasn't sure he'd be strong enough to withstand the torture again.

Would she still care for him if she knew how weak he really was?

It didn't matter, because he would ensure he was never again tempted by pain to release his power and endanger her and her kind. Even if it meant isolating himself from everyone for the next five centuries, or however long it was until death came for him, if Mother Nature would be so merciful as to take him before the end of his natural life cycle.

After climbing unsteadily to his feet, he placed the washcloth in the sink, turned and hesitated in the doorway. With his back to the woman who had given him so much, he murmured, "I have to leave."

"Quinn, whatever happened in your past—"

"I can't change," he said. *But I can do something about the future.* "Thank you. For everything." Quinn walked away, noting the absence of footfalls behind him, and feeling the crushing weight of loss with every step that he took.

His fox howled at the idea of deserting their mate, but Quinn could see no other alternative. He wanted so much to surrender to the promise of security Manning had offered earlier, but couldn't bring himself to accept it. Manning may have been able to look past his dual heritage because he was the *Aucinthe*, but that didn't mean the man's tolerance would extend to the rest of the *Vam'kir* race. Quinn would give anything to know if Manning could truly be trusted with the potentially devastating power he harbored, but he just couldn't take the risk.

It's better this way. Though he couldn't help but wonder at the back of his mind if he might, one day, actually come to believe that.

Chapter Ten

Fatigue lived deep within the marrow of Manning's bones, sapping his strength and robbing him of fortitude until all that was left was a man grasping at the seams of helplessness. Not since his mother's death had he felt so powerless over the order of his life, only then he'd had the force of rage to balance his grief. The blame had sat solely on his enemy. Now that he was the one at fault, he found the very fiber of his morals called into question.

Manning scraped a tired hand over his face as he entered the living room. George and Adan looked up from where they sat on the couch, his father rising slowly to his feet.

"Is he awake?"

"Yeah," Manning answered gruffly. "Merebeth's talking to him now."

Adan rifled a hand through his black hair, dark eyes glittering with guilt. "I should have told you sooner. We all should have done something—"

"No. I won't let you take responsibility for my mistake. I was the one who called Armand without

Quinn's knowledge. I ignored the signs, thinking I knew what was best for him and almost cost him his life." His throat constricted over the admission and he had to look away, unable to bear the reflected truth in his father's eyes.

George cleared his throat and stood, breaking the tension of the moment. "I'd say I warned you but being as how I know what it's like to be in the doghouse, I'll let this one slide. However, I think it goes without saying that if my mate hadn't interfered, I'd have kicked your ass."

A corner of Manning's mouth lifted despite the severity of the situation. He was still sporting the scars of their brief clash, in no way disillusioned about the potential outcome had Merebeth not used the power of her voice to freeze them into immobility. As the historian of their race, she was the only one whose authority surpassed even that of the *Jaes'dins*.

He'd always been aware of that fact, but the why of it had never clicked until she'd divulged, along with the reason for Quinn's existence, her friendship with the historian of the *Vam'kir*. They were, essentially, the designated keepers of the *Aucinthe*. Working together and empowered by *Miel se Luuda* to teach and protect the chosen against both races so that he might choose his own path without bias and prejudice. They alone understood it mattered not which race prevailed, but that it was the use of the power the *Aucinthe* held that would win the battle and decide the fate of the Mother's creation.

Manning tipped his head in acquiescence to the older shifter's statement. Eventually during the fight, he would've come to his senses and remembered to use his own authority to end it, but not until after a substantial amount of damage had been inflicted.

George stood and walked around the couch to clasp Manning's shoulder. "Having said that, I only have one word of advice. Kneepads. Get a pair and use 'em well. Best investment I ever made."

"Kneepads?"

"Gonna take a lot of groveling to keep your boy here," George clarified as he headed for the kitchen. "Padding makes it easier on the knees."

Manning grunted, hoping he could get as far as groveling. Quinn seemed as resistant now as he'd been in the beginning. Unless Merebeth could pull another one of her miracles and keep his mate from running again, Manning would be back to chasing him.

"Son, the Alpha and your *Ketai* will be here soon. You'll need to explain what's going on. Merebeth knows they're coming, so if anything happens, she'll back you up, although I don't think that'll be necessary."

No, it won't, Manning thought grimly. Because if any of them tried to harm his mate, hormones or no, it would be the last chance they ever got. "Have you told them anything yet?"

"Only that they were to talk to no one about what happened until speaking to you first."

"Thanks, Dad." He didn't particularly want to talk to his men and the Alpha, not with his relationship hanging so precariously in the balance, but knew he couldn't put it off any longer. They waited together outside and were joined five minutes later by Cain, Tailor, the Alpha and his four Betas. The men stepped out of their cars looking disgruntled and more than a little confused, but lacked aggression.

Manning stepped down from the porch to greet them, noting how Tailor and Cain took up positions at his sides, silently stating their allegiance. It was a credit to their loyalty that they would stand by their *Jaes'din* even while being no more informed of the situation than the others, and Manning expected nothing less from his *Ketai*. Still, he was grateful. Armand also took this in and wisely showed no offense to their actions.

"*Jaes'din*," Armand respectfully inclined his head, as did his men behind him.

"Armand."

The other man looked to the front door and back again. "Your mate?"

"He's fine. Alive." Some of the tension left his body at Armand's sincere expression of relief.

"Look." Armand scraped a hand through his short, brown hair. "We came here to apologize first and foremost. I honestly don't know what happened. As soon as Adan answered the door, my men said they smelled something and lost control. I should've reacted sooner, but I know they would never intentionally harm your mate—"

"I know," Manning said. "If any of you did, you'd be dead." He paused to let that sink in, meeting each man's gaze with the harsh impact of his own. They weren't his enemies, but he needed them fully aware of the consequences, should they abuse the knowledge he was about to impart. "I don't hold you accountable for what happened, but I will for what I'm about to tell you. Speak of this to anyone and it won't be banishment you'll be facing."

The Betas exchanged nervous glances, but Armand remained steady, a subtle nod his only reaction to the none-too-subtle threat. Manning went on to give them a shortened version of the true history of their kind, their relation to the *Vam'kir* and Quinn's unwitting standing in all of it. When he was done, uneasiness thickened the long silence that followed.

"Speak," Manning ordered.

One of the Betas fidgeted then began hesitantly, "Sir, if he was raised *Vam'kir*, how can you be certain of his motives?"

"What motives are you referring to, Reece?"

"I just think it's a little odd that he showed up so soon after the disappearances and the first coordinated attacks we've had from our enemy in a century."

Manning ground his teeth, bristling at the insinuation yet knowing the suspicion was legitimate. "He's been living in the States for three years and came here expecting a job and nothing more. It was Merebeth who convinced him to stay and we both believe he wasn't involved in the attacks."

"So what do you plan to do with him?" Armand asked.

"I plan to let him make his own decisions. I'll not force him to bond with me."

"He doesn't want to bond with you?"

The incredulity in the man's tone ate away at his patience. "If your mate were *Vam'kir*, would you readily give them a power that could be used to destroy your own kind? He has a right to his wariness, and as he pointed out to me earlier, our kind has committed acts just as heinous as those of the *Vam'kir*."

"But if he remains unmated, he'll always be a target," Reece began, looking to his fellow Betas as though searching for concurrence. "I mean, I scented his arousal and it was like I was under some kind of compulsion. I would've done anything, gone through anyone to get at him. It was insane —"

Manning growled and took a step forward, his panther snarling protectively within. "Tread carefully, Reece."

The other man paled considerably, eyes widening.

Armand held up a quick hand in placation. "I think what he means to say is, who exactly are we protecting Quinn from? I'm assuming that since he's not with his own race, he doesn't trust them, and we can't risk them taking him now that we know what he is. On the other hand, if he remains unbonded, we're just as much a threat to him."

Manning sighed heavily. "I don't have any more answers than you do at this time. He's...secretive." To say the least. "But I do know I won't lose him. If he chooses not to stay, we'll take turns protecting him from a distance. I'll contact the Alphas of the nearby communities and have them send in a few of their Betas and warriors to watch over the town while any of you are gone. You'll be accompanied by either me or my *Ketai* at all times. If this happens, Quinn is not to be approached unless his life is in danger. As for the issue of the attacks—"

Cain cleared his throat loudly from behind, causing Manning to look back in time to catch Quinn's furious expression peeking out from the screen door. His mate disappeared in the next instant and Manning sped after him, forgetting about the other men entirely. He skidded to a halt at the entrance to the apartment where he watched Quinn struggle with the locked doorknob then twist it sharply. The mechanism gave way with a dull crack and his mate slammed through the door then stomped to the bedroom.

"Quinn..."

Quinn pulled a suitcase from the closet, flipped open the lid and started throwing clothes into it from the dresser.

"Where are you going?"

His mate flashed a glare that somehow managed to contain sarcasm, rage and annoyance all at once. "What does it matter? You'll follow me anyways, won't you?"

"Yes," Manning hissed, feeling the last of his patience dwindle with every scrap of clothing that hit the suitcase on the bed.

"Why?" Quinn shouted. "Why won't you let me go?"

"Because you're my mate."

Quinn barked out a humorless laugh. "So you think I'll give in because of my hormones? You think I'll give you the power to control my kind?"

"I've never thought that," Manning growled. Fuck if the man didn't infuriate him to no end!

"You think I'm going to turn around and bond with one of my own kind and give them my power?"

"No," he ground out through clenched teeth, not quite sure if the blood roaring in his ears was owing to anger at the accusation or stark fear.

"Then why are you going to have me followed like I'm some criminal?"

"Because I love you!" he shouted back. "I've already lost my mother and my father's as good as dead. I *will not* lose you, too."

Quinn stopped to stare at him, face flushed and mouth open. Manning cursed his foolishness immediately, inwardly berating himself for a job well done. Not only had he chosen the perfect time to confess his feelings, but he was doing so to a man who, it seemed, had an intimate fear of commitment.

At any second, he expected Quinn to finish packing and leave. To his surprise, however, his mate merely sat on the bed, his shoulders hunched in as though his energy had suddenly deflated.

"I am the son of the *Magnique*. Second son but still a prince." Quinn turned the weight of his tortured gaze onto Manning, his gray eyes dry yet swimming with emotion. "When my spirit matured, my father knew what I was. I thought..." He swallowed hard. "I thought he hated me because I was part *Ba'Kal*. That he was punishing me for being gay and having a spirit, but he knew."

"Sweet Mother." Manning scrubbed a hand through his hair. "Quinn, I know—"

"No, you don't know! I could've killed you!" Quinn took a shuddering breath then averted his gaze to the window. In a whispered voice almost too low for Manning to hear, he said, "He kept me locked up for four years. Tried to force me to mate with a man of his choosing. Someone strong enough to force me to unlock my power so they could use it together in battle but also a person he could control. I wanted to die. I wanted to give in and I hated myself for holding on. When my sister found me, I hated her at first for saving me. I was scared of everything, scared of my own erection." Quinn laughed breathlessly then hung his head in his hands. "Now I find out I could've been responsible for the annihilation of an entire race if I'd given in." After several seconds he turned again to Manning, lashes tipped with unshed moisture. "Tell me again that you love me."

It was Manning's turn to swallow heavily. His fear. His pride. The unmitigated fury that rolled through him like a hurricane unleashed. What Quinn was speaking of— Manning knew the act of bonding between mates was the same for *Vam'kir* as it was for *Ba'Kal*. The union required sex as well as the exchange of blood. To endure years of forced subjugation of the basest kind— To be abused by his family, his own race, was— Manning's vision blurred as his cat howled in outrage. His gums and knuckles ached with the need to release his spirit and draw blood, but he reined in his instincts.

Slowly, he walked to the side of the bed and knelt before Quinn without touching him. Words of vengeance, love and promised safety froze in his throat as he stared into his mate's eyes. They were full of doubt and self-contempt, but they met his without wavering. The realization hit him then that Quinn wasn't simply searching for acceptance, he was searching for a solution. What good were answers if they did nothing to fix the problem?

"Get up. We're leaving."

"What?"

"I want to show you something. Just us. It'll only take an hour. If you still want to leave afterward, I swear I won't interfere." When Quinn's gaze darted to the suitcase, he added, "Do this for me and I won't fight over custody rights of Penche." Perplexed disbelief erupted into a breathy laugh and Manning grinned in return. "I'll understand if you want Merebeth to go as well. I'm sure she wouldn't mind."

Quinn deliberated for several moments while gnawing on his bottom lip. Finally he shook his head. "I'll go without Merebeth."

"Thank you." As they stood, he caught Quinn's arm as his mate swayed precariously. "Do you need more blood?"

Quinn looked up at him sharply, mouth opening in silence as though at a loss for words. "That...doesn't freak you out?"

After adjusting to the concept of a male mate, being rejected, discovering love and learning that his mate is the *Aucinthe...* "I think I can handle it."

Besides, he'd be a hypocrite if he couldn't. During the first day after Quinn's attack, it had been he who'd donated blood several times to replace what had been lost. The sight of his mate's physiological reflexes kicking in at the scent of life giving blood, the feeling Quinn's fangs piercing his wrist and the gentle pulls of his mouth, had been nothing like what he'd expected. The entire process had felt as natural as anything he'd experienced with Quinn. More than natural, gratifying.

"I'm okay, but what about your men?"

"I'll talk to them later. I'm sure they've left by now." Manning's suspicion was confirmed as they walked around the cottage and found the front empty but for their own cars. They climbed into Manning's, and Quinn kept his gaze riveted on the scenery outside as they traveled. Dark wisps snagged in the stubble along his jaw and kept most of his face hidden from Manning's view, but the turmoil of his agitation seemed subdued.

Fifteen miles from the outskirts of the other side of the community, Manning drove through the abandoned streets of his town's original settlement. He began speaking of the town's history, as much to break the strained silence as to lure Quinn from his brooding. When the community had formed in the area approximately two centuries ago, its members had culled a piece of land just large enough to accommodate their small numbers. In time and prosperity, they'd outgrown the boundaries of the settlement, yet were reluctant to cut down more of the wild vegetation.

Opportunity had struck in the form of calamity when a natural forest fire had cleared a stretch of land fifteen miles to the east sixty years ago. The community had moved, but the ghost remnants of their once lively village still remained.

Manning pulled up in front of an old, two-story bungalow at the end of a row of houses. From the look of curiosity and wonder on his mate's face, anticipation melded with the hope that bloomed in his chest that this last-minute plan might hold worth after all. His mother's old house was such a simple thing bordering the outskirts of an abandoned community, but it held a wealth of significance for him, and he prayed that his mate would let him share it with him.

He killed the engine of his car and got out without a word, knowing Quinn would follow. The quaint dwelling was constructed completely of stone walls with hardwood flooring. Overgrown plants and weeds hid much of its unique architecture and protruded from multiple cracks in the mortar. The planks of the wraparound verandah creaked in protest beneath his boots as he stepped to the arched doorway.

Inside, layers of dust and cobwebs filmed the cover sheets over furniture interspersed throughout the entire open first floor. Unobtrusive pillars had been erected to lend support to the second floor, which consisted of two bedrooms. The house was run-down and weather-beaten, but it still held an echo of the happiness that had once lived within it.

"Wow."

Manning hid a smile at the awe in his mate's voice. Quinn ran a hand almost reverently over the plantation-style shutters in the living room then crossed to the large fireplace to gingerly touch the oak mantle above it.

"This is where my mother grew up," Manning spoke quietly. "When Adan came to claim her as his mate, she refused to leave. She was an orphan by then and didn't want to give up the house her father had built for her mom, so he moved in with her. I was born and raised here until I was about nineteen and the community moved to preserve the forestry. Like a lot of its members, though, she couldn't bear to see it torn down. 'There's magic here', she would say."

"It's beautiful."

"Yes, it is," Manning murmured, seeing only his mate. A well of emotions pooled in his gut as he forced his next words out. "I'm leaving in two weeks."

Quinn jerked around, brows drawn in confusion.

"There have been more murders, and I think they're the same trancers — *Vam'kir* — who are behind the disappearances of our kind and the murder of my mother. The attacks appear deliberate. Methodical. There have been…messages left behind. I need to find the ones responsible before more are killed."

With a hesitant nod, Quinn cleared his throat. "Why two weeks from now?"

"I need to fix this place up first. Make sure it's suitable for you to live in." As shock registered on his mate's face, he added, "I won't force you to stay, but I may be gone for months, even years. I need to know that no matter what happens, you'll always have a safe place to come home to. I'll notify my *Ketai* and the Alpha that this area is to be restricted from all other visitors."

"I can't accept this," Quinn said, shaking his head and taking a step back.

"I've already signed over the deed with Merebeth and my father as witnesses. It's yours, if you ever want it."

Time lengthened as Quinn continued to stare in disbelief. Manning stood his ground, ready to counter any further argument.

"What about your line? Going after the murderers could start a war whether you want it or not. Will you be...?"

Manning thought he caught a glimpse of moisture on his mate's lashes before Quinn showed him his back.

"Will you beget an heir before you leave?"

The air was punched from his lungs at the mention of the forgotten issue, the only argument for which he hadn't been prepared. Securing his line was what he should do, what he'd set out to do in the search for his mate, but without Quinn there to complete the family, it felt like an utter betrayal. A violation of the sacred bond between mates he'd been raised to respect.

Manning strode across the open expanse separating them, spun Quinn around and took fierce possession of his mouth. There was resistance at first and, for a brief moment, Manning wanted to rip himself away, but the call of the predator inside was too great. When he felt the tension against his body recede, he backed his mate to the nearest wall and held him there, pouring every ounce of his emotions into the heat of his mouth and the firm touch of his hands. For all of Quinn's strength and independence, his astonishing intelligence and compassion, he could be an amazingly selective listener. Manning couldn't let him leave without believing the words he'd committed to earlier.

Pulling back, he rasped, "There will be no family without you."

Quinn stared up at him in mute surprise for so long it felt as though an eternity had passed. Then a single tear fell from red-rimmed lashes. "No bonding," he whispered.

Manning shook his head. "I have all I want right here." A low groan rumbled through his chest as Quinn threaded fingers through his hair and pulled him down to bring their mouths together again. This kiss was searching and desperate and blazed through his blood like wildfire.

How could there be anything better than this? The feel of his mate surrendering to him against all odds, and the passion-laced fervency that gave him a rush like no other. He could wait, for a year, a decade. However long it took for his mate to realize the truth of his intent.

Chapter Eleven

Quinn lowered his arm after coating the last patch of the ceiling with white paint, rolling his shoulder to ease the stiffness. A smile stretched his lips as he looked around at the walls of the living room. He'd painted them all, being relegated to the job as he knew nothing about home repairs, and was proud of his accomplishment. It felt good to work with his hands and see the fruits of his labor come to life. After only one week, the natural beauty of the bungalow had been restored and Quinn thought the transformation matched the residual joy he'd felt in it upon his first arrival.

A dull ache pierced his chest at the reminder that he would be the only one enjoying it for some time. He couldn't go with Manning when his mate left to fulfill his duties, and wasn't sure he wanted to even if he could. That Manning loved him was evident in everything he did, from the way he held him at night to the possessiveness in his eyes when their gazes met. Quinn couldn't deny anymore that he cherished it all, but the ghosts of his past still haunted him like chains around his heart. Chains that steadfastly refused to allow him to let it love again. And if he did cave to love and fall to the temptation of bonding? No. It was too dangerous. More than his heart rested in the balance of his decision.

A grunt caught his attention and he looked to the doorway where Armand and Cain were carrying in a roll of carpeting for the upstairs bedrooms. Being the only two mated out of the lot who knew of Quinn's secret, they'd readily offered to help. Cain enthusiastically, using it as an excuse to spend time away from his mate. Quinn had met her a few days ago and her gruff demeanor was so much like her mate's it was small wonder they bumped heads constantly and aggressively, but he had felt the love between them. Deep and abiding.

He switched his gaze to the sight of the man in the kitchen working underneath the sink. Manning was on his back with only his lower half in view. His black T-shirt was pulled up, showing an expanse of hard-toned midriff between its hem and the loose-fitting jeans slung low on his hips. Sleek ridges rippled and contracted as he fought with the piping, making Quinn's mouth salivate with an urge to run his lips over the fine dusting of hair that covered them.

He leaned a little farther to get a better view and sucked in a breath as his hand slipped from the top of the ladder he was on. Unable to stop his backward momentum, he tried to twist his body as the floor came rushing up. The air was punched from his lungs when strong arms caught him just in time to keep his ass from an untimely demise. The paint tray followed him down and again he was saved as Armand snatched it out of the air just before it could land on him. A loud growl came from his right and he looked over to see Manning stalking toward them, teeth bared in a snarl.

Cain lifted Quinn to his feet and snarled right back. "Don't get pissed at me, man. You're the distraction that caused him to fall."

Quinn ducked his head as a furious blush crept over his cheeks. "Thanks," he mumbled, taking the paint tray from Armand, who wasn't helping with the wide grin on his face.

Manning turned him around, ignoring Cain, and tilted his head up. "Are you okay?"

More heat rose and he tried to brush his mate off, but Manning held firm. "Fine. I'm fine." This was hardly the first time he'd been caught ogling his mate, and doubtless wouldn't be the last. Manning smiled and bent down to faintly brush his lips across Quinn's mouth, bringing forth a wash of desire that had Quinn melting into the arms that slowly surrounded him. He opened to let his mate's masterful tongue tangle with his in a sweet dance of lust and passion.

"Get a room," Cain growled from somewhere in the distance.

"Get a life," Manning responded without breaking contact.

"Tell that to my mate. And, while you're at it, tell her you need me to work this Thursday night when her parents come over."

Quinn and Manning both chuckled and broke apart. Manning took his shirt off and used it to wipe the sweat from his brow. "It's getting late. Let's call it a day and meet back in the morning."

Adan trotted down the stairs, rifling dust from his hair. "Sounds good, but I'm bringing the grill with me. I've eaten more sandwiches this past week than I have in the past decade."

Quinn grinned. "I'm done with the painting. I'll cook if you bring the steaks."

"No," Manning said quickly.

Quinn widened his eyes and smacked him in the gut. Hard. The man refused to let go of the time he had burned the chicken, and the burgers, and the pizza that was supposed to be fail proof but apparently wasn't.

"I meant I can do that while you figure out where to put the furniture. You wanted to decorate, right?"

The rest of the men laughed as Quinn narrowed his eyes. This discussion wasn't over. They packed up their tools and secured the house then went their separate ways. Manning gave Tailor a call on his cell as he drove them both back to Merebeth's to let his *Ketai* know they were finished for the day. Tailor, being unmated, had done the only thing he could and stood guard at the entrance to the main road running through the abandoned town to keep young pups from adventuring into it, as they apparently had a habit of doing. Manning wanted to be sure his edict that all shifters refrain from the area was obeyed.

As they skirted the community, Quinn's gaze traveled to and fixed on the sight of his mate sitting beside him. Arousal bloomed deep in his groin as his gaze roamed over tanned flesh and corded muscles. Manning had said that he'd noticed Quinn before he'd ever taken in his scent, but it was still hard to believe. Quinn was bigger now, but they were still like night and day in physical appearance. What the man saw in him was baffling, but he no longer wanted to question his opinion, not when his mate made him feel as though he was just as attractive.

On a whim, Quinn unbuckled his seatbelt and leaned over, pulling one of Manning's arms from the steering wheel to slide in and take one of his smooth nipples into his mouth. The taste was salty with sweat and the small disc puckered as he sucked it in, rolling it between his teeth then swirling his tongue to sooth the sting. Manning hissed and clenched a hand in his hair but didn't pull him away.

"What are you doing?"

Quinn moved farther in to work on the other nipple, biting down just hard enough to cause the abs beneath his hands to bunch, then sucking it. "I'm finishing what you started earlier." He flicked the nub with his tongue while he lowered a hand to Manning's emerging erection and squeezed it through the denim.

Manning groaned and threw his head back. "You're killing me."

With a soft chuckle, he unfastened his mate's pants and gripped the straining shaft that popped free. "Just keep your eyes on the road, big man." A hint of uncertainty made him pause and glance up. Manning was all about safety, and what he had planned didn't exactly fit into that category, but the shaded look of stark desire in his mate's eyes quelled any doubt that he wanted this.

After Quinn took the initiative once more, he resituated his body and dipped down to lick the pearly drop of pre-cum from the slit of the flared head then wrapped his lips tightly around it. The feel of the member swelling in his mouth and hand, the strong scent of his mate's arousal hitting his senses, was an aphrodisiac that pounded through his blood. His own cock filled with the surge of his answering pleasure in the rough confines of his jeans. He ran his tongue around the tip and slowly began taking the full length into the heat of his mouth, reveling in the feel of

Manning's hand pushing down on his head until his lips were pressed to the thick patch of hair at the base.

The way Manning asserted his dominance always gave him a thrill. It was tentative at times and utterly compelling at others, but never more than Quinn could handle. If anything, Quinn had found there was a certain level of power in the way he let his mate take charge. The knowledge that Manning would stop everything in a heartbeat or increase his sensuous control with just a look from him made him feel alive with passion and need.

When the pressure at his head eased, he built his own and hollowed his cheeks as he drew up then took his mate's shaft to the root again. He did this repeatedly, humming around the stiff length while deep moans from above filled his ears. These sounds cranked up his arousal until his cock was pulsing painfully against the zipper of his pants. When the urge to relieve the ache became too much, he maneuvered one of his hands to his crotch and fumbled with the button of his jeans.

Manning tugged his wrist away and held onto it. "Don't even think about touching that. It's mine."

Quinn groaned and retaliated by working his throat muscles around the head of his mate's member then rising to squeeze just beneath the head with his lips. Manning rocked his pelvis as much as he could in the seat and pushed down on the back of Quinn's skull again, forcing him to swallow the shaft whole.

"We're almost there, baby. Fuck, don't stop."

Less than a minute later, the car came to a jerking stop and Quinn barely had time to take a breath before the hand in his hair pulled him up and Manning's tongue replaced the cock in his mouth. His mate drowned him in a searing kiss that ended abruptly as the man jumped out of his side of the car then walked around in a purposeful gait. He was yanked out of the passenger side door and lifted into a strong embrace. As he wrapped his legs around his mate's waist, long arms crushed him close and his mouth was once more plundered by that clever tongue.

"What about Merebeth and George," he managed to get out.

"Won't be back...till...later," Manning said between devouring kisses. He walked them around the cottage to the apartment then kicked open the front door.

Quinn laughed breathlessly. "You're gonna have to fix that."

"Add it to my list."

As soon as they were in the bedroom, Quinn gasped as he was thrown onto the bed. The heated look Manning latched onto him sent a shiver down his spine, and it was all the encouragement he needed to scramble out of his clothes while Manning did the same. From the top drawer of the nightstand, his mate pulled out the latest bottle of lube and poured it liberally onto his fingers and cock. Over the past week the man become somewhat of a connoisseur of lubricants, testing out every single brand he could find in town until he'd found the perfect one. It'd made Quinn laugh, but truthfully he was only grateful he wasn't with his mate for the purchases. Feeling his lust spin out of control when they were around others was bad enough.

"Turn over, pup. On your knees," Manning said, voice rough with desire.

Quinn complied and raised his ass in the air, body trembling in anticipation and raging erection dangling between his open thighs. Warmth surrounded him as his mate climbed onto the bed behind him and lay over his back to trail kisses across his skin. Then Manning sat on his heels and with one hand still smoothing over Quinn's back used the fingers of his other to rub over the crease of Quinn's entrance before pushing in.

The pressure on his sensitive nerves made them clench convulsively, and when a second finger was added and they hooked forward to graze along his prostate, Quinn grasped the blanket and rocked back, emitting a low keening that was beyond his will to contain. A third finger joined them and the magic they worked as they forked in and out, brushing up against his sweet spot with each pass, had his cock twitching with need.

"Please, please," he called out, unable to stand it any longer.

Manning growled and withdrew his fingers, aligning the head of his cock with Quinn's quivering hole. "I love it when you beg for me." In one powerful thrust, he buried himself to the hilt, gripping Quinn's hips in a merciless hold.

Quinn cried out at the burn and sheer ecstasy of being taken by his mate. Flames licked over his skin as he was speared over and over again by the thick shaft of his mate. It'd been so long, two days since the last time they'd made love, and it felt like an eternity. Between the preparations for Manning's departure and the restoration of the bungalow, they hadn't had the time or energy for more than hurried blow jobs. He didn't know when he'd become such a sex fiend, but the quick fixes were never enough to satisfy him. He craved the feel of his mate embedded so far inside him they seemed to meld into one being, the assurance of Manning's body sinking into him and surrounding him with the pleasure they created.

Fire spread through his blood and rushed to his groin as his fangs threatened to explode from his gums. Manning pumped into him harder, quickening his strokes and hitting his prostate until sparks lit underneath Quinn's flesh. The tide of his orgasm rushed through Quinn as his balls pulled in tight. He arched his back and shouted out his release, his cock erupting in streams of thick cum. Manning leaned down and clamped his jaws onto Quinn's nape, grunting as his own climax filled the channel that was milking him dry.

The teeth that eventually released his neck should've alarmed Quinn, but instead they made him feel secure. Content. No canines had pierced his skin and the restraint Manning showed when they made love always held him in awe. Not many mates could resist the lure of bonding, but Manning had never wavered from his promise.

Manning pulled out and tumbled to the side, taking Quinn with him so that they lay spooning each other. "I love you, pup."

Quinn felt his breath catch, wanting to return the sentiment but not quite able to. Not yet.

And what if he never returns?

No. He wouldn't think about that. Maybe, when he was ready, he would seek Manning out, but until then...

A loud thud came from the front of the apartment followed by pounding footsteps. Manning was on his feet before Quinn could even sit up, moving to the foot of the bed between his mate and whatever threat might show itself, but it wasn't a threat. Mara appeared in the doorway, flashing blood red eyes and baring fully extended fangs in a look that promised death.

Oh shit! What the hell is she doing here?

"Mara, no!" Quinn shouted.

But it was too late. His sister leaped across the room in one bound to tackle Manning, but the man had already shifted to his panther form. The sleek cat dodged her extended nails then spun around, launching itself at the same time Mara turned her body. Huge paws shoved her to the ground on her back and the cat's jaw stretched to clamp down on her throat, hard enough to hold her immobile but not enough to break skin. Mara screeched and slashed her nails across the panther's ribcage, leaving deep furrows in their wake.

"Stop this!"

Quinn jumped from the bed and snatched one of Mara's wrists in his hands, but in her blind rage, she twisted her wrist and slashed at his chest, laying the skin open in a wide arc across his breastbone. A scream was ripped from his throat at the searing pain that tore through him, but he forced his mind away from it, changing tactics to wrestle Manning from her prone body. The scent of his blood must've triggered their senses, for the next thing he knew, Manning was crouching in his human form with one arm curved to cage Quinn in behind him while the other was outstretched to ward off any further attacks.

Mara sprang to her feet and tensed into a fighting stance but remained still. "Release my brother," she snarled.

"Your...brother?"

For the first time Manning took his eyes from his target, if only briefly, to cast a questioning glance back at Quinn. His gaze lit with alarm on the blood pouring down Quinn's chest, but Quinn backed away before he could touch him, glaring at them both and holding a palm to his lacerated flesh.

"Manning, Mara. Mara, Manning. I would've introduced you two on better terms but... Oh wait, that's right. You were both too busy trying to kill each other."

"Quinn," Mara started, "what the hell's going on here? The stench of shifters is all over this place. Your front door is busted open and I come in to find you naked with one of the...the creatures." Her eyes widened as if in realization. "Was he trying to rape you? I swear to Miel se Luuda if you hurt my brother—"

"Whoa, wait, just hold on," Quinn said as Manning growled dangerously. "It's not what you think. Manning would never hurt me. He's my... My..." His mind went blank, at a loss as to how to explain Manning's role in his life. Manning looked back at him and he thought he saw a flash of pain in those fathomless eyes before they fell again on Mara.

"His boyfriend."

"Your *what?*"

"Is it safe for me to come in now?" All heads turned to the door at the sound of Cassie's voice.

"Yeah, Cassie," Quinn called. "You can come in."

Mara had no choice but to climb over the bed to get to her mate as the blonde walked with trepidation into the room. Her blue eyes brightened when she saw Quinn and Manning then widened in shock just as quickly. A hand flew to her mouth and she giggled through it. "Oh, my God, we caught you in the act, didn't we? Wow, I would say sorry but damn, Manning. You look good in the buff. You too, Quinny."

Mara placed herself between them and her mate and frowned. "You know this guy?"

"Of course. He's the boyfriend I told you about when I came back from my visit. He's as harmless as a kitten."

Manning groaned at the poor and untimely reference then turned and pulled Quinn up with him. Quinn winced as his skin stretched but was grateful for the arms that locked around him. His head was spinning with the adrenaline still flooding his veins.

"I need to take care of my ma—boyfriend," Manning corrected himself. "You can wait for us in the living room."

Mara bristled visibly at the authoritative tone, but Quinn nodded quickly, letting her know it was all right. After the women left, he was guided by the arm to the bathroom and lifted to the countertop while Manning took a washcloth from a drawer. Quinn struggled for words, anything to break the tense silence between them, but came up with a whole lot of nothing. He sat uncomfortably, barely noticing the pain as his mate cleaned the shallow gashes on his chest then dried them with a towel until they no longer bled. After Manning took care of his own wounds, Quinn opened his mouth, needing to say something, but was stopped by the gentle press of lips on his.

"I'll excuse myself and let you talk with your sister."

"No." Quinn reached up to grasp Manning's head, looking into his eyes. "Please stay. I want you here." Reluctance shone in his mate's eyes and for a moment, Quinn thought the man would deny him, but Manning merely nodded in acquiescence. After getting dressed, they walked to the living room where

Cassie was staring worriedly from the recliner at her lover who was pacing in front of the couch.

Mara stiffened then went to stand beside her mate. "Quinn, what are you doing here? With him?" She pointed an accusatory finger at Manning.

Quinn sighed and took hold of Manning's hand then walked around to the front of the couch where they sat. He could lie, there wasn't a doubt in his mind Manning would go along with it, but he'd seen the tortured look in the man's gaze when he'd failed to claim him as a mate earlier. The love he'd shown Quinn deserved better than a dark corner in a small closet.

He took a breath to gather his courage then said, "Manning is my mate, and... I think I love him." Manning's head whipped around, his eyes searching, and Quinn could only send him a pleading look. He wasn't sure, not truly, but it was the only way Mara would accept their relationship. Manning seemed to understand this and gave an almost imperceptible nod.

"This is a joke right? Are you out of your mind? He's a fucking shifter!" Mara cried out. "I can't believe you would do something this crazy! That *thing* is our enemy!"

Cassie sank her face in her hands as Mara continued her incensed tangent, spouting invectives and waving her hands as her voice grew in volume. Through it all, Manning sat stoically, though Quinn knew what it must've cost him. The condemnations that flew out of his sister's mouth about shifters were even starting to get on his nerves, but he waited patiently for the downpour to fizzle out.

When it was over and Mara stood tapping her foot expectantly, he said quietly, "Are you done yet?"

"Not if you don't give me a damned good reason not to rip him to shreds."

Quinn let out a sigh. He knew that beyond the betrayal of keeping this a secret from her, his sister merely feared for him, and he couldn't blame her in the slightest. From her eyes, this situation would've scared the shit out of him, being too similar to the one she'd rescued him from years ago. But this time no coercion was involved, and she needed to understand that. "This was my choice, and I can explain it if you'll let me."

Mara visibly reined in her anger and gave a barely perceptible nod.

He calmly explained to her the truth of his situation, leaving nothing out. Not even his speculations on why their father had subjected him to four years of torture. He made sure to include the fact that this was his home now, and that Manning had no intentions of ever forcing him to bond.

If his mate was moved by any of it, he never let on.

By the end, though, Mara's pale skin had turned ashen and she sat heavily on the arm of the recliner. Quinn shared a frown with his mate then looked back to his sister. "Mara, I promise you that I trust Manning. He won't force me to bond and use my power against our race."

Cassie's reaction wasn't much better. Tears glistened on her lashes, painting trails that reflected the light as they spilled down her cheeks. A petite hand went to her lover's arm and squeezed it as if in support.

Mara shook her head and took a deep breath. "I believe you," she whispered. "Every word. It explains everything." She stood and began pacing again then stopped abruptly to face them. "Father's searching for you. Here, in the United States. And so is Antoine."

"What!" Manning surged to his feet, his sudden anger making even Mara flinch. "How do you know this?"

"He came to my house in Sacramento looking for him. I think he knows that I was the one who stole Quinn out of France because my brother disappeared right after I left from my last visit there and I haven't been home since. It's been three years, but I think he's been searching since then. He mentioned interrogating a few shifters, but I didn't understand why until now. It makes sense, if he knew Quinn was part shifter all along."

Manning exploded in a roar that shook the windows and had both women shrinking away from him. "He killed them. He killed them all just to get his precious *Aucinthe*," he spat out.

Mara shook her head in confusion. "Killed who?"

"My mother, and two others. He even had the grace to leave behind a message written in blood saying, 'Surrender him'."

The women gasped in unison. In a tremulous voice, Mara said, "I would never...think it of him, but I know what he did to my little brother. I'm sorry for your loss."

Several minutes of strained silence went by then Manning spoke up again. "I'm assuming you came here to warn Quinn, and that you told your father nothing."

"Of course," Mara responded in a slightly indignant tone. "My father may be the *Magnique*, but he commands no respect from me. Quinn has always been my first priority. My protector stayed behind to make sure we weren't followed from the airport. She'll join me here shortly."

Manning nodded and turned to Quinn. "Do you have any idea where he might look for you next?"

Quinn gave no answer, his mind having retreated the moment his tormentor's name had passed his sister's lips. He could see everyone in the room from a distance, hear their words faintly as though through a tightly meshed filter, but was unable to respond. Memories flitted in a macabre dance along the edges of his consciousness, toying with reality and threatening to crush his tenuous hold on it. He didn't want to feel, didn't want to think past what he knew had to be done. If he slipped… If he slipped, the world would come crashing down around him and he would be back in his tormentor's barren room, in the dark, where his existence was only known to the two men who wouldn't let him die.

"Quinn?" Manning asked, but the sound brushed by him like falling leaves in the wind.

"I have to go," he murmured, standing as if on autopilot and heading to his room. Manning clutched his arm and turned him around. He stared up into the familiar face of his mate but didn't quite see him.

"Quinn, don't do this."

He frowned as his body was shaken roughly by hands on both of his arms. "You won't stop me. You promised."

Manning growled and shook him again. "I will not let you run from me now. I can protect you."

Quinn gave a humorless laugh. "No. I'll protect you, all of you." When he tried to turn away, another set of hands gripped him and Merebeth's face replaced Manning's, her eyes unyielding as they seemed to bore right into his mind.

"Come back, *Aucinthe*," she spoke imperiously, her tone taking on an odd cadence that vibrated through Quinn's skull.

Her powerful voice ripped him from the precipice of his memories and plunged him back into awareness so fast his head reeled with the crushing impact. His knees gave out, but it was Manning who caught him. Manning who held him as his body shook with sobs and tears streamed unchecked down his cheeks. All he could do was hold on to his anchor through the storm of his emotions and pray that when it ended, Manning would still be there.

Chapter Twelve

"He loves you, you know."

Cassie's words barely registered in Manning's mind. He was still caught in the threat of Quinn's father out there, loose in the Ba'Kal territories. A madman bent on destroying the one being who represented the only hope for peace between their races. The vision of Quinn's horrified expression when he'd learned his father was hunting him had filled Manning's nightmares over the past two days. More than that was the chilling resolve of his mate to leave behind everyone he loved to protect them.

It made Manning sick to think how close he'd come to losing his mate all over again if it hadn't been for Merebeth's interference.

"Manning?" Cassie asked.

He steered his gaze away from his mate with effort to peer over at her. She sat in the lawn chair next to his and placed a cold beer in his hand. After pinching the bridge of his nose, he took a long swig while mulling over her words. "What makes you say that?"

The woman shrugged a shoulder and looked skyward. "Oh, I don't know. Could be the fact that he's still here."

"That was Merebeth's doing."

"Not really," Merebeth disagreed, taking a seat on the other side of him. "I pulled him back from the edge of disaster, but it was you who kept him grounded."

Manning looked back to his mate, the ache in his heart not diminishing with their words. Quinn was sitting at a picnic table in the backyard of Manning's mansion surrounded by Adan, Mara, Cain and Armand, along with their mates. His hair gleamed blue-black in the bright, afternoon sun and his pale features were highlighted by the faint color in his cheeks, thick eyelashes and full lips red from worrying them incessantly between his teeth over the past few days. When Quinn threw his head back and laughed at a joke, Manning's breath caught in this throat. It was the most gorgeous sight he'd ever seen, yet he could feel the strain it took for his mate to act normally and see the shadows behind his gray eyes that hinted at the trouble within.

"When Mara brought him over from France, we had to take shifts watching over him," Cassie said. "Even broken as he was, he was still so independent." She gave a short burst of laughter and pointed the tip of her beer at her lover. "He even tried to sneak away once in the middle of the night. Mara was so furious she rented a cabin out in the middle of nowhere for some one-on-one alone time with him and had Shannon camp outside to stand guard in case he tried it again."

Manning frowned, his attention peaked. "Did it work?"

The blonde shrugged, but her eyes twinkled with merriment as she looked over at him. "I don't know. Apparently the kitchen burned down only three days into their hiatus and they had to come back early."

A slow smile began to curve his lips. "He tried to cook, didn't he?"

Cassie hid a grin behind her beer that still managed to seep into the rest of her delicate face. "I'm not at liberty to say."

Manning's laugh was cut off by a sharp poke to the ribs.

"I hope you fireproofed the kitchen in that bungalow of his," Merebeth said in a tone that was no less than a warning.

"Umm... Yeah. George and I are going to finish up with it tomorrow." *How the hell did one fireproof a kitchen?* Simple. Remove all threats from the area and everything would be fine. In this case, it would be his mate, but he wisely kept that remark to himself.

His attitude sobered when he realized the bungalow would have to remain empty for some time. He was one step further in catching those responsible for the murders and, most likely, the kidnappings, but the identity of the mastermind behind them pushed the possibility of war straight into the 'no shit' zone, and Quinn was the link to it all. At the moment, Manning's place was the safest for him to be. He would need to find those of his warriors who were mated to guard over it while he was gone, then somehow convince Quinn to move in.

Should be a cakewalk.

Manning rubbed at the growing headache behind his temples. "Listen, I want to keep Quinn here for the night unless either of you have a need of him." Mara had insisted on staying close to her brother, taking the living room in Quinn's apartment for herself and her mate to sleep, and while Manning held no objections, he also thought a little alone time for both parties would relieve some of the stress that had been building.

Both women shook their heads and Cassie smiled knowingly. "I think that's a great idea. Oh wait, do you guys have toys there? We had to leave ours behind."

Manning choked on a swallow of beer and cleared his throat. "Uh... Sorry. We're fresh out." Not a chance on earth he was telling her about the stash he had hidden in the back of the bureau in his room. He had no idea what Quinn would think of it, but he'd find out... One day.

Cassie pouted then perked up in the next instant. "Hey, I remember seeing a store in town that sells them. Merebeth, wanna come with us to do a little shopping?"

The older woman lifted her brows and cocked her head to the side. "Actually —"

"And on that note, I think I'll go check on the burgers." He made a quick escape and hovered near George next to the grill for the remainder of the get together.

By early evening, the house was empty but for Adan, Manning and Quinn, as well as four mated warriors standing guard at the front and back of the grounds. There was a listlessness to his mate's movements as he led him to the bedroom, but he knew better than to push. Quinn would come around in his own time. He gently pushed his mate to sit on the foot of the bed then knelt at his feet to remove his shoes.

"I'm sorry about your mom."

With an inward sigh, Manning mastered his expression before looking up. He'd known this was coming. Quinn was too compassionate to leave the burden of his father's sins resting on the shoulders it belonged to. "What happened is not your fault. It's not the blade that is dangerous, but the person who wields it."

"And what if the blade wants to wield itself?"

Manning blinked at the first sign of true emotion from his mate in two days. Palpable, righteous anger wafted from the man's energy in waves. "What are you saying?"

Quinn stood and strode to the curtained window by the dresser and paused for long seconds. When he finally turned around, determination lined every inch of his frame. "I want to go with you."

There was no question as to what he was referring to and Manning's chest swelled with pride. Slowly, he gained his feet but kept the distance between them. "That's not possible."

"The hell it—"

"Not unless you're bonded," Manning said. "I can't afford to divide my men." It was a harsh reality for them both, but one that needed saying. From Quinn's expression, Manning could tell his mate was calculating his next argument, and it caused Manning's gut to twist in apprehension. "No. If you think I would allow you to do that, you're a damn fool."

Quinn's face flushed with anger as his hands clenched at his sides. "It's my decision to make."

"Not without my assent."

"You're going up against my father. You could die!" Quinn shouted.

"I will not allow you to dictate your life by his rules!" Manning shot back. "I want you to bond with me on your terms, not his." He took a steadying breath then said, "If I die, I'll leave this world knowing that you live." When his mate opened his mouth to protest, he overrode it with a curt gesture. "No more. That is *my* decision."

Pain lanced his heart at the tears brimming on Quinn's lashes, but they didn't fall, and he refused to take back his words. The impact of what his mate was willing to sacrifice to save him from potential death was staggering, but that's all that it was, a sacrifice. And he would be no better than the monsters of Quinn's past if he were to accept the bond his mate was offering.

Manning stripped out of his clothes and tossed them to the floor then walked around to the head of the bed. As he drew back the covers, he said, "Come to bed, pup. We'll discuss our plans in the morning."

Quinn caught his bottom lip between worrying teeth and creased his brow in agitation before defeat finally won out. He crossed the room and let Manning help him out of his clothes. Together they climbed under the sheets and Manning pulled his mate into the protection of his arms, waiting for sleep that wouldn't come.

* * * *

Manning threw back the duvet, sat up and scrubbed the dry grit from his eyes. A glance at the alarm clock showed it was past midnight and, with a sigh, he slipped on a pair of flannel pants then padded down to the kitchen. His mind was waging a war on three fronts with no end in sight. Meetings for strategic maneuvers would begin in the morning and there was still the issue of an heir to carry on his line, but it was Quinn's offering above all that hammered at his thoughts relentlessly. Without his power, hundreds could die on both sides, yet at the same time, if Manning took his power for the sake of war, it would be no different than what the *Magnique* had set out to do once he'd realized his son's potential.

When did the violence and manipulation end?

With a sigh, he poured himself a double shot of whiskey, downed it then poured another. He was caught in a perfect catch twenty-two and found it left a very bitter taste in his mouth. He stood lost in thought for some time, staring out of the new window pane above the kitchen sink. Just as he was about to fill the glass with a third shot, a scream sounded from the direction of his bedroom. He slammed the glass down and raced back to find Quinn sitting up in bed. His eyes were wild and tendrils of sweat-drenched hair were plastered to his sheet-white face. Manning willed the panicked beat of his heart to slow and hurried to the bed, taking his mate into his embrace. Quinn trembled uncontrollably with the aftereffects of whatever had shocked him awake.

"Shh, it's okay. Just another dream," he soothed. One of many Quinn had been suffering from since learning of his father's recent actions, or maybe it was the same one over and over again. He never spoke of them, and after his breakdown, Manning was reluctant to pry.

Quinn pinned him with a desperate stare, fully aware now. "We have to go back. I need to check on my sister."

"She's fine, baby."

Quinn shook his head adamantly. "I have to know. Please."

They held each other's gazes for several seconds before Manning turned on a sigh to grab his cell phone from the nightstand. "I'll give her a call, all right? What's her number?" As Quinn recited the digits, he punched them in and waited for Mara to pick up. When she didn't answer, he tried again to the same effect. "I'm sure she's just sleeping," he offered in an attempt to reassure his mate, though a sliver of his own distress had wedged its way into his chest.

"I can go," Adan said from the doorway, his face and clothes rumpled from sleep.

"Sorry, Dad. Didn't mean to wake you."

Adan waved it off with his usual aplomb.

"Manning," Quinn cut in. "I need to go."

The determination Manning so admired was shining from his mate's eyes and he knew the younger man wouldn't let it go. At this point, he doubted any of them would be able to find rest regardless. "All right, we'll take my car."

They wasted no time dressing and loading into the car. The trip was strained and the anxious energy Quinn was exuding from every pore made them all nervous. It wasn't until Manning was halfway down the dirt road leading to Merebeth's cottage, however, that he began to give merit to his mate's worries.

Something was wrong.

Through the vents in the vehicle, he detected the faint, sickly sweet smell of old blood. The flood of headlights as he pulled up revealed nothing out of the ordinary except for the gaping doorway showing ominous darkness within. Even so close to the community, Merebeth never left her door unlocked at night. The moment Manning opened the driver side door, the scent of decaying blood slammed into him like a brick wall.

"Stay here," he ordered Quinn. "Let me scout the place first."

Without waiting for an answer, he shifted to his feline form and approached the house warily, pricking his ears for any signs of life. There were none. Not even the lulling sounds of the forest animals could be heard above the ringing silence. He made a swift circuit of the perimeter but again came up empty. Whoever had come had also left by way of auto transportation, for there were no scent trails leading into the woods.

When he came back around to the front, he saw his father chasing after Quinn who was already running up the front porch and into the cottage. Manning shifted back with a curse and followed them in, then immediately froze as Adan turned on the living room light.

The entire scene was painted in grotesque shades of red. Where once ordered chaos had reigned now resided the twisted signature of a madman. Furniture was upended or shattered completely and the walls were splattered with blood. The one opposite him caught his attention first. On it was written the same message that had been delivered at the previous murder sites — *Surrender him.*

Nausea burned at the back of his throat as he took in the bodies strewn across the floor. Merebeth lay in a maroon puddle with limbs akimbo and amber eyes staring vacantly up at the ceiling. One outstretched hand was held by her mate who lay face down at the end of a large smear of blood, as though he'd tried to reach her with his last dying breath. A woman he didn't recognize lay several feet away, body bent backward over the upturned side of the coffee table and pale face exposed to his horrified view. Even slack with lifelessness, Manning could tell she'd been a warrior from her muscular frame and placed her to be the protector Mara had spoken of.

"Son, we need to—"

"Quiet!" Quinn whispered. He lithely made his way around the scattered debris, his shoes making sucking noises through the pools beneath them, and headed into the kitchen. Manning and Adan went with him to find Cassie curled into a tiny ball in the far corner. Quinn rushed over and rolled her gently to her back, cradling her head in his lap. As her blonde curls tipped in red were brushed back from her face, her lids fluttered slightly but wouldn't open, as if she were fighting for the life that Manning could tell was fading fast.

Quinn sent him a look that seared itself into his very soul. "Get an ambulance."

"Already on it, son. We have a medic in the community," Adan said, dialing a number on his cell phone. "We'll have to take her to his clinic. Will you be all right to go?"

When Quinn nodded, Manning strode over to pick the woman up only to stop when his mate snarled fiercely at him. He knelt down and held his hands out in a pacifying gesture. "I'll give her back to you once you're in the car. You have to trust me."

Quinn blinked and shook himself. "Sorry."

"Don't apologize. Wait, we should find Mara."

"She's not here," Quinn said in a voice that was frighteningly hollow. "I would've felt her."

Manning ground his teeth but managed to bridle his anger. There would be time enough for that later. When his mate eased back, he lifted the small body into his arms and carried Cassie outside. Though her clothes were torn and soaked through with blood, no open wounds were apparent. At the car, he handed her over to his mate in the back seat and closed the door, watching as Adan sped them toward the clinic in the middle of the community.

He took his own cell phone from his back pocket and called his *Ketai* and the Alpha, keeping the information to a minimum until they got there. A cursory scan of the apartment showed no signs of forced entry or damage, and neither were there any clues as to where Mara had been taken, or if she'd even been present at the time of the attack.

With nothing left to do until the others arrived, he stood silent vigil over the dead at the front of the cottage and clung with all of his strength to the anger that was saving him from the turmoil of his despair.

* * * *

"Mara."

Quinn started at the soft whisper. It came again and he lifted his head from the edge of the bed to the still form lying in the middle of it. Only Cassie's head was visible above the line of the dark green duvet. Her usual halo of brassy curls lay flat around her colorless face, her eyes dull as they searched sightlessly for her love. He rose to retrieve an ice chip from the cup on the nightstand and rubbed it along the seam of her chapped lips. Her gaze when it met his was haunted, and it was all Quinn could do to hold his composure as large tears rolled down her temples.

"You're safe now. It's okay," Quinn crooned, but she only shook her head weakly.

"They t-took her. They took my baby."

He shut his eyes for just a moment to steel himself against the tide of emotions her simple words evoked but instead, was jarred by a flash of the scene from the night before. He'd known instantly that Mara wasn't in the cottage, but she had been. Some of the blood that had coated the walls had been hers, carrying her unique, floral scent.

Cassie began to heave with broken sobs and Quinn quickly reached beneath the covers to grab one of her hands as she tried to wrap it around her broken ribs. He placed it over the duvet and checked the needle adhered to the back of it.

"We'll get her back, sis. I swear it." But her sobs only worsened. He opened the top drawer of the nightstand and took out the syringe the doctor had given him for just this purpose.

"No, wait." Cassie batted limply with her other hand, making him pause. "Your f-father was there. He gave me a message for you."

Quinn stilled, not sure he wanted to know but compelled to listen.

"He took her to F-France. He's going to give her to Antoine in one week if you don't go back." Her voice began to elevate to such a high pitch, it became hard to understand her. "I'm so sorry, Quinny! I love her, but you can't go. She could never live with herself if she lost you. She's gone now. You can't go…"

Cassie repeated the words over and over again until they ran into each other like watercolors under a fine mist. Quinn uncapped the syringe and slowly plunged the sedative into the tube, leaning forward afterward to press a kiss to her forehead.

He felt as though the world was slipping away, as it had done three days ago, as it had always done during the darkest hours of his imprisonment. Freedom was easily found in withdrawal, and he had claimed it once, but then Mara had come and forced him to face the light again. Now she was the one who would lose herself to the emptiness, the only escape from Antoine's sadistic torment.

She would resist, and she might fail, but she was a fighter.

And so the fuck am I. Manning hadn't wanted him to join the battle against his father, but he could see little choice now. His mate and his sister needed him, and he would play his role in the upcoming war whether they wanted him to or not. But first he had to talk to Manning, and that meant finding him. With Cain under orders to keep him at the mansion for protection, convincing the *Ketai* to take him to his mate would be impossible. He'd have to get past the guard somehow if he were to carry out his plan.

An idea came to mind and he shouted, "Cain, come here! I think something's wrong!" He ran to the dresser to grab the heavy ceramic lamp on top then stood just behind the open door. Seconds later, Cain pounded in and Quinn swung, bashing the lamp across the back of his head. The big man fell to the floor with a loud thud. Quinn pushed him over onto his back to check his vital signs. No real damage, but Cain would have one hell of a headache when he woke.

"Sorry, buddy." Guilt speared him, but he quickly banished the emotion. Time was of the essence and he still needed to provide a diversion to slip past the men Manning had posted outside. He raced to the kitchen, snatched up the nearest appliance and threw it at the window. The sound of the glass shattering faded behind him as he ran through the living room to the large foyer. He opened the front door just in time to see the guards disappearing around the side of the building to investigate the disturbance. His spirit answered his call with enthusiasm, lending its form and giving him an extra boost of courage. The moonlit grass flew beneath his feet as he sped across the open lawn to the road and beyond that, the line of trees.

Chapter Thirteen

Manning had told him an hour ago that he was going to the Alpha's house to meet with the others and formulate a plan of action. From past experience gained watching his father, Quinn knew that could take all day, if not several. With his *Ba'Kal* gifts combined with those of the *Vam'kir*, it wasn't hard to pick up the freshest trail of the Alpha's scent. Quinn tracked it through town, staying to the shadows as much as possible. Few people were out this late and none saw him. When he came to a dead end at a four-story building, he retraced his steps and doubled back twice. A winding road that curved up a steep hill brought him to a huge, Victorian-style house with several cars parked out in front. The building wasn't quite as large as Manning's mansion but close enough in size.

He could smell the alluring scent of his mate as he neared the entrance but called on his years of self-discipline to tamp down the effect it had on his body. Manning had forbidden him to come to the meeting for reasons both justifiable and not, but those reasons had ceased to matter. His mate was about to learn that this war was no longer his alone to bear.

Swiftly, he shifted back and walked in through the front door, following a muffled uproar of voices through the foyer, an expansive sitting room, and down a long hallway to the right. The narrow space housed doors on either side, but it was the far one that contained what he was after, the one with a bald shifter with Cain's width and Manning's height standing guard outside of it.

Well, skittles. Quinn grinned as Cassie's favorite saying popped into his mind. Apropos, considering his newfound strength was owing to her.

The guard unfurled his arms as he saw the newcomer and took a step forward. Quinn called his other shift into being and let his fangs and nails drop, his vision flowing to red. As expected, the shifter morphed into his animal state and gave chase. Quinn spun around and put on a burst of speed, racing back through the house. As soon as he was out of the front door, he leaped up and grabbed onto the overhang, lifting his legs in time to hide above the massive wolf that barreled out seconds behind him. When the shifter stopped at the bottom of the porch to search for his lost prey, Quinn jumped down and ran back inside, locking the deadbolt just as the door vibrated under the weight of the wolf crashing into it on the other side.

He used his speed again to run back to the room, knowing the shifter would find another way in soon. At the door to the meeting room, he pushed a little too hard, forgetting to subdue his strength, and winced inwardly as the door crashed reverberating against the wall.

But the distraction served its purpose.

What must have been at least twenty shifters sitting around a large, oval table turned to stare at him, with more lining two other sides of the room. Quinn didn't realize he was still in his *Vam'kir* form until half of them pulled knives from hidden sheaths and the other half shifted in preparation to attack.

"Stop!" Manning's voice boomed, and at once everyone froze. Everyone except Quinn.

He shifted back and looked over at the head of the table where his mate stood, body coiled with rage. In his fury, Manning was an impressive sight, and one that held him pinned in place. Slowly, Manning walked around the table and advanced on Quinn, his hand shaking slightly as it fisted the hair at the back of Quinn's skull and yanked lightly, forcing his face up.

Sweet Mother. He loved the control his mate took over him. Manning's power was intoxicating and went straight to his groin, but Quinn held his desire in check.

"What are you doing here?" Manning ground out.

"I need to do this." Quinn set both palms on his mate's chest and pushed away until the man finally dropped his hand and took a step back, puzzlement replacing some of his ire. "Tell your men to back down." For a moment, he didn't think Manning would. Not because Quinn was intruding upon a meeting where he wasn't welcome, but because he was afraid for his mate. Quinn could smell it on his scent and see it in the faint trembling of his hands, and the knowledge made his chest clench tightly.

Then Manning turned to the men and used the voice of the *Jaes'din* again. "No one here will touch this man or in any way do him harm. If you try, it'll be the last mistake you make. Put your weapons away and resume your positions."

Every man obeyed the order, including the guard outside that had returned, though Quinn could see that some were fighting the compulsion. When his mate looked back to him, he took a deep breath and gazed out over the rapt audience. With Manning keeping no less than a foot of distance from him, he neared the table and saw a large map of the United States spread out on its surface, with a map of France underneath. The men closest moved abruptly away as he reached out to switch the maps so that the one of his native country lie on top.

After taking a moment to scan it, he pointed to the town with which he was most familiar. "This is the location of the *Magnique's* clan, thirty miles from the town of Florac. It's his base of control with his fortress in the center. There are smaller clans surrounding it on all sides that are no different than the community here, making it necessary to go through innocents to get to him." Quinn glanced at the men who were now leaning over to peer at his finger on the map.

"That is not where we're going, however. A few centuries ago, his grandfather restored a great castle here." He pointed to another spot about a hundred miles to the northwest. "And fortified it for defensive means. Since then it has been expanded and made stronger so that today, it's nearly impossible to breach, but there are tunnels that run the length of its underbelly leading to various points of entry. They've been long out of use and caved in at the access points but we can dig through to a few of them without being seen or heard. We can infiltrate the castle through these and attack from the inside. I'll draw a map of the inner structure and point out where most of the guards will be positioned."

He looked around again, satisfied with the interest on many of the faces in attendance. "Any questions so far?"

A man with graying hair spoke up. "How do you know all of this?"

"Because I'm the son of the *Magnique*."

Angered voices rose in a sudden cacophony that grew to a deafening crescendo until Manning shouted above them all. "Silence! He is not our enemy."

"He could be leading us into a trap," another said.

"He would no more lead us to our doom than I would," Armand countered.

"Are you saying you trust him?"

Without even a hint of hesitation Armand nodded. "I have seen for myself the sort of man he is, but if you don't believe me, maybe you'll believe your own eyes." He turned to Quinn and dipped his head with a gleam in his eye.

Understanding dawned on Quinn and he looked back at his mate, who seemed to also agree with a slight nod. Quinn took a few steps back and reached for his spirit, then let the change come over him. From his new vantage point close to the ground, he watched the men scramble over each other in an effort to get away, their shocked cries and curses filling the air. When he changed back to meet each of their bewildered gazes, the room erupted into another bout of vocal chaos until Manning once again quieted them.

"You may have a spirit," the gray-haired man said, "but you're still a trancer. Do you honestly expect us to believe that you're turning your back on your race and aligning yourself with *us*?"

"I'm not aligning myself with you." Quinn turned to face Manning. "I'm aligning myself with my mate." The beat of wings whispered in his stomach at the slow smile that curved Manning's lips. More outraged denials and curses rang out, but they weren't nearly as loud now.

Armand cut them off with his next sentence. "Quinn, why would you have us go to France? All of the clues lead us to believe that he's still here."

He was briefly grateful for the man's discretion in keeping his father's true goal from the others. Without looking away from his mate, but loud enough for the others to hear, Quinn said, "Cassie was given a message. My sister will be forfeit in one week unless something is done." He could tell only moments later that Manning had ascertained what he wasn't saying by the return of fury in the man's dark eyes. For those that couldn't understand, he added, "And this is the only way to prevent the war my father will bring to us if we don't act now. No more need to die than is necessary."

An uncomfortable hush fell over the crowd, during which Quinn never broke away from his mate's intent gaze.

"I will vouch for him, and I'll go," Armand said as he stood.

"As will I," Tailor called out. The Alpha's four Betas stood and chimed in their assent as well, followed by Adan.

"And I," Cain said as he walked in with a hand cupping the back of his skull. "Damn, little man, did you have to hit so hard? Next time just pull out a gun and shoot me. It'll hurt less."

Heat rose in Quinn's cheeks and he grinned sheepishly. "Would it help to know I apologized afterward?"

Cain grunted as Manning lifted a brow in question, to which Quinn merely shrugged. A few more assents followed, but Quinn wasn't paying attention to the men anymore.

Manning pulled him close and leaned down to whisper, "If your sister is there, there's a chance your father will kill her before we can reach her. Are you sure about this?"

Yeah, he'd thought about that, but the answer was simple. "I trust you."

* * * *

Quinn stared sightlessly at the diagrams on the low accent chest before him. He'd drawn every detail of the castle he could remember and had gone over every possible scenario of the coming battle but still had the persistent feeling he was missing something. He was positive Shannon hadn't revealed the fact that Mara was hiding his location, which meant she'd come of her own volition like his sister had promised. It also meant his father must have followed Mara and Cassie here. If that were the case, however, he had to have seen Manning hanging around the cottage and suspected he was the *Jaes'din* and more powerful than the average shifter. Otherwise, why would he have waited until they were gone to attack?

Was he counting on Manning to follow Quinn to France, making this one big set-up?

Quinn tossed the pencil down and massaged his temples. He should be asleep but was too afraid to close his eyes. The only way to keep the images of the scene at the cottage at bay was to keep his brain occupied. Hours had passed since he and Cain had departed from the meeting room and left Manning to deal with the confusion and solidify the plans, and there was no telling when his mate would return.

A soft knock at the door made him jump and he looked over to see Cain coming in with a plate of food. Quinn summoned a watery smile, thankful the man didn't hold a grudge against him for his earlier stunt.

"How's she doing?" Cain glanced at the bed.

Quinn looked at Cassie's still form wrapped in the thick duvet and sighed. "She ate a little bit but went right back to sleep. Doctor said it's normal after a concussion."

The other man nodded then set the plate down in front of him. "I noticed you didn't make yourself something to eat so I brought you a sandwich."

"Thanks, but I'm not hungry."

"No offense, but my man hits harder than you do. He comes back here and finds out you haven't eaten and it's my ass."

Quinn chuckled then a thought occurred to him. "Hey, do you know if Manning has a laptop I can use?" From it, he should be able to access Merebeth's accounts and convey the news of her death to her contacts. Not exactly something he particularly relished doing, but he hadn't been there for the burial. An effort to see to her business affairs was the least he could do, and waiting until he returned from France would be too late.

Cain cocked his head. "I think my old one's still in my room."

"You have a room here?"

"I live here."

Quinn's jaw dropped at the knowledge then he recalled his first visit to the mansion during the full moon. Manning had commented that the others were gone, preferring to spend that time with their families. Guilt speared him as he realized what Manning had done. For him. "Tailor lives here as well, doesn't he?"

"And the guards outside," Cain confirmed.

Why hadn't he thought of it before? Manning was the *Jaes'din*. He had to have his *Ketai* and guards close for protection and convenience. The *Magnique* had an entire fortress full of men and women under his personal service, yet Manning had emptied the mansion of all but his father to keep the unbonded *Aucinthe* safe.

"I'm sorry. I didn't—"

"No worries, man," Cain said, waving off his sentiment. "I'd do the same for my mate. Any of us would. You still want that laptop?"

"There's no need," Manning cut in.

The scents of pine and musk permeated Quinn's senses and he looked over to see his mate standing in the doorway. His jaw was shaded with stubble and lines etched into the corners of his eyes added to his haggard appearance, but the sight made Quinn's body thrum with excitement.

"Come here."

Quinn stood from his chair, barely noticing Cain's hasty retreat, and followed Manning as the man turned and headed for the bathroom. He could feel the low hum of agitation from his mate and tried unsuccessfully to banish the impression that he was a recalcitrant child being led to his punishment. All of the justifiable reasons he'd formulated for doing what he'd done scattered as Manning closed them into the bathroom and sent him a quelling stare. His mate wore his power around him like a cloak, and the effect had not gone unnoticed.

"Get undressed."

Quinn shivered at the low tone and complied as Manning did the same. His mate turned on the shower and adjusted the temperature then pulled him in. As soon as the stall door closed, Manning was on him, backing him to the wall and holding him there with the press of his huge frame. Large hands weaved into the threads of his hair and he looked up in time to see the smoldering depths of Manning's yellow eyes before his mouth was taken in a demanding kiss. When he tried to duel with the tongue that swept across his, it only plunged deeper, dominating him with every pass. The smells of pine and musk grew stronger until Quinn felt as if he were drowning in it.

Manning's hands began to travel everywhere, skimming down Quinn's chest and spanning over his stomach. Their path trailed fire over his skin and sent blood rushing to his groin. His cock filled with sudden urgency as those hands quested lower and squeezed the mounds of his ass, bringing their pelvises together. Manning's erection ground hot and hard into his abdomen, sliding against Quinn's as he swiveled his hips.

When his mate guided his arms above his head and held his wrists against the wall with one hand, he didn't question the action. He could only relent under the heat of Manning's encasing body and the sweeping strokes of his tongue. The other hand moved to his chest and he gasped as one of his nipples was pinched and rolled between two fingers. The flash of pain seemed to meld with his pleasure and he arched his back, wanting more, needing more. Manning did the same to his other nipple, teasing it relentlessly to a hardened nub.

Quinn could hardly think straight as he was spun around and his hands guided back to their same position on the wall.

"Keep them there," Manning ordered in a husky tone.

The smell of Manning's ocean-scented body wash filled the air seconds before Quinn felt a slick finger slide down his crease and probe his quivering entrance. The digit drove in at the same time Manning brought his other hand around and fisted Quinn's aching member. Quinn cried out at the dual sensation, bowing his head to watch the hand on his cock ease from base to tip in a tight grip. A thumb rubbed across his slit with every upstroke until the pace quickened. Another finger was inserted and his hips started to move of their own accord, thrusting into the clenching fist then impaling his hole onto the fingers that worked its sensitive ring.

He could feel his orgasm rising swiftly but wanted his lover inside him, stretching him impossibly. "Manning, please," he begged.

Manning pulled his fingers out and squeezed the base of Quinn's cock as he leaned in close. "I can't be gentle right now, love."

The words made Quinn's rigid member swell even more in its tight confinement. "I don't want you to be."

The response was immediate. Manning used a foot to spread both of Quinn's, his hands to pull Quinn's hips back and expose his puckered entrance. Quinn trembled with anticipation and, when his mate's thick cock speared him, driving in to the hilt, his breath caught in his throat. He hadn't been fully prepared, and the pain was consuming at first, but then Manning began to move and pleasure overrode all other sensations.

His mate's shaft pounded against the walls of his channel as the grip on his hips increased, digging into his skin and pulling him back with each powerful lunge. He would have bruises in the morning, but they'd be worth it. He loved this about his mate. Even in the beginning when Manning had treated him with glass fingers, afraid to push too hard, Quinn had sensed the predator in him—the wild aura that could never be tamed by rules or expectations. And, when he let go like he was doing now, it made Quinn feel like he was flying, free of everything but the strong embrace of the man's unyielding control.

Manning bent lower, changing his angle so that his swollen head grazed over Quinn's prostate, sending coils of heat blazing to the pit of Quinn's groin. He was so close, the pressure within building like a raging inferno.

"Harder," he breathed. "Fuck, I'm gonna come."

"Not yet. Not until I give you permission," Manning growled.

A shiver coursed down Quinn's spine at the gruff edge to his mate's tone. *Sweet Mother*, he could come from the man's dominance alone. He gasped as Manning pulled out and he was spun around again and lifted by the waist. Instinctively, he wrapped his legs around his mate and grunted when his back hit the wall and cool tiles met with the heat of his skin.

"Look at me," Manning ordered. The moment their eyes met, Manning slammed himself deep into Quinn's channel, eliciting a sharp cry. "Don't ever put your life at risk again."

Each word was delivered with an aggressive thrust, the hands on Quinn's waist giving him no option but to take every inch of his mate's considerable length, and it was all he could do to hold onto the man's shoulders and keep his legs in place.

"Answer me, Quinn," Manning demanded. "Tell me you'll never do that again."

He found it nearly impossible to focus, but when his gaze met Manning's, he was lost. There was such raw need staring back at him it seemed to burn into very his soul. No one had ever looked at him like that, like he was the center of their world, and his heart constricted with a whirlwind of emotions. He needed this man, craved everything about him and...loved him. The unbidden thought made his eyes prick with moisture but Manning gave him no quarter.

The pace quickened as Manning growled, "Quinn—"

"Never," he whispered. "I promise." His mate pumped furiously then and Quinn could no longer hold back the tide of his orgasm. "Please, please..."

"Come for me."

And he did. Quinn screamed as his climax bowled through him, his cock bursting forth ribbons of cum between them. It seemed to go on forever, milked by the driving thrusts of Manning's pulsing member. A roar echoed off the walls of the stall as heat filled his clenching channel. Manning took his mouth again in a passionate kiss that stole his breath and caused his cock to twitch with aftershocks.

When Manning finally lowered Quinn's feet to the floor, his knees threatened to give out and he was saved only by the arms that banded tightly around him. His mate pressed their foreheads together and they stood like that for countless minutes.

"I need you," Manning whispered.

The words that had passed through Quinn's thoughts earlier were on the tip of his tongue but wouldn't come out. Soon. He would say them soon, but not yet. All that he'd learned in the past week still weighed too heavily on his mind. "I need you, too."

When Quinn's legs could hold him again, Manning washed them both, taking his time even though Quinn could feel his exhaustion. In the bedroom, they dressed discreetly and Manning grabbed the plate of food while Quinn checked on Cassie before following him to another bedroom. His mate insisted he eat the entire sandwich, which he did with a lopsided grin at the order, then pulled him into the bed and tucked the covers around them. Sleep came like a soothing balm, free of nightmares and undisturbed until the morning light.

Chapter Fourteen

The airport terminal was bustling with life and energy that tested his nerves and made his skin crawl with irritation. He'd always hated crowds, and the fear of them that had been installed long ago didn't help matters.

"Relax," Tailor spoke quietly beside him. "Want me to get you a shot?" He jerked his head toward the bar of the small restaurant they were in.

Quinn thought long and hard about that, seriously tempted to give in, but eventually shook his head. He couldn't afford to lose even an ounce of control over his libido with Tailor there. Manning had told him that they would go to France first to get everything situated with hotels and travel accommodations. Armand and his Betas would fly in the next day, along with the warriors from every other community that could make themselves available over the next few weeks, which according to Manning was quite a bit. Quinn had warned his mate of his misgivings, but Manning had assured him they would take all precautions before setting their plan to action.

Cain smirked at him from the other side of the table and said, "I could hit you over the head with a lamp. You wouldn't feel a thing till you woke up."

Quinn grinned evilly. "Only if I can shoot you afterward."

Tailor sat back with a huff. "I always miss the good stuff. Next time you pull something like that, little man, make sure I'm there to see it."

"Sorry, you're shit outta luck. Promised Manning I wouldn't do that again." He laughed softly as Tailor grumbled something under his breath and Cain flicked a cube of ice from his drink at the man. His leg started to jitter impatiently and he took a deep breath, which also didn't help. *How long did it frickin' take to book passage for five people?* Manning was still at the ticket line reserving seats for Armand and his Betas on the next flight to France. They couldn't risk touching each other with Tailor there, but the absence of his presence was just as irritating as the crowd around him.

Quinn's gaze began to wander over the sea of people rushing to unknown destinations when something caught his eye. A man. He was familiar in a way that was both comfortable and alarming. The sea swayed, hiding the figure for a moment, and when it became clear again, Quinn's heart went into overdrive.

It was his brother, Rowan. More than seven years had passed since he'd last seen the man, but he would know him anywhere. They could've been twins except for the distinct difference in their sizes. Rowan was everything their father had wanted in a son, and at eleven years Quinn's senior, the next in line for the throne. Rowan crooked his finger at Quinn, beckoning him, then was gone in the next instant.

"Are you all right?" Tailor asked.

"Huh? Yeah, just want to get out of here is all." *Think, Quinn. Think.* Rowan appearing out of nowhere so soon after Mara's abduction had to mean he knew something about it, but his brother would never approach him so long as he sensed shifters around. The thought that Rowan's presence might be part of a trap touched his thoughts then fled just as quickly. The brother he remembered was nothing like their father, and he couldn't imagine Rowan associating himself with their father's schemes. Perhaps Mara had notified him of the *Magnique's* intention of finding Quinn.

Deciding that had to be the case, Quinn scrambled to find a way to ditch his guardians. In his gut, he knew Manning would never allow him to meet with his brother, even if it gave information that could benefit them. His mate was too cautious, too protective to allow for such a risky move. And Quinn couldn't lose this one chance of discovering what his father's real plans were.

Manning's gonna kill me for this.

"Umm... I'm going to go buy a book or something. Keep my mind busy."

"I'll go with you," Cain said, standing.

Quinn slanted him a sly grin, hoping it hid the nervousness churning in his stomach. "I'm a big boy, Cain, but if I run into trouble, I promise to scream like a little girl."

Tailor burst out laughing, but his remark got the desired response. Cain sat back down and pointed a finger at Quinn. "No more than ten minutes. Manning should be back by then."

Quinn nodded and walked over to the bookstore kitty corner to the restaurant. He went in and pretended to browse, disappeared behind one of the casements and waited for a good minute to pass. Cain and Tailor were talking animatedly among themselves when he peeked out and dashed out of the store, for the first time in his life grateful for the mass of flesh moving around him and hiding him. He took off in the direction he'd last seen his brother, turning a corner that led to a dead end with elevators on either side. He took one down to the lowest level, figuring Rowan would want to talk to him in an area where he could make a quick escape if Quinn happened to have shifters with him.

The doors opened and he walked into the underground parking lot, which was surprisingly empty considering the crowds in the terminal above him. A quick scan didn't reveal his brother, so he followed the trail of Rowan's scent and started on the path to the right, a feeling of unease descending upon him with every step. When he was almost at the doors of the next entrance into the airport, a man jumped out from behind the enclosure and grabbed his arm. Another stepped out as well, with his brother a few feet behind, but it was the man restraining him that held all of Quinn's attention.

Terror flooded in and seized his chest until his lungs refused to take in air. *This isn't happening. This isn't happening,* his mind screamed at him, but that didn't stop Antoine from crushing Quinn's back to his chest, trapping his arms at his sides and covering his mouth with one hand. Survival instincts kicked in and Quinn fought against the hold like a man possessed, kicking his feet and butting his head in a vain attempt to get away. A black limo with tinted windows pulled up beside them and the second man opened the back door for Antoine.

Quinn struggled harder but to no avail. He was carried into the back of the limo where Antoine sat, and was forced into his lap. Still, he fought while voices buzzed around him, distant under the roaring in his ears. The moment the hand was removed from his mouth, his hair was wrenched back and fingers dug into his cheeks, prying his jaws open. More fingers pinched his nose and a cold gush of fluid shot down his throat. Quinn choked on the blood pouring into his mouth but had no choice but to swallow it. It raced through his veins like rampant tendrils of fire, spreading the drug it contained throughout his system until he could think of nothing but the consuming pain.

Then the agony slowly faded, taking with it Quinn's ability to resist. The hands fell away, all but for Antoine's, which resituated Quinn so that he was seated between the man's legs. His head lolled but was held in place by a deceptively gentle hand. Nausea roiled in his stomach at the feel of an iron erection pressing into his backside but there was nothing he could do about it. He knew the drug they'd given him and had felt its effects many times in the past. It was a type of narcotic to humans but an inhibitor to *Vam'kir*, which allowed its victims to feel, see and hear everything but rendered their bodies powerless.

His gaze roamed over the other occupants of the limo and another flood of terror washed over him. Two men sat on either side of Antoine with his father directly across from them, and a third to his left. Royce, the *Magnique*, appeared just as Quinn remembered him. Black hair pulled back into a slick ponytail and faint lines around the corners of his steel gray eyes the only testament to his century and a half of life. He was slightly shorter than his eldest son, who stood at six foot three, but their large frames were identical.

"You look good, Quinnten," Royce commented with false amiability. "I'm glad to see you've been taking care of yourself, or is this new look of yours owing to the shifter you've been fucking?"

Quinn glared at his father, mentally screaming every curse he couldn't form into words.

"It seems you've forgotten where your true loyalty lies, but no matter. That will be rectified soon. We're going to finish what we started so many years ago and, this time, you're going to obey without question."

Quinn wanted to laugh at his father's audacity.

As if reading his thoughts, Royce said, "Don't worry. I'm not going to force you, and neither will Antoine. You're going to submit all on your own. You see, I've had plenty of time to prepare for this in your absence. Your brother is, at this moment, seeking out your lover and explaining to him that searching for you will have dire consequences indeed. He's being told that all of the prisoners I've taken over the past year are being held at an unknown location in France and that if he dares to come after you, my men will kill every last one of them."

Oh, Mother, the disappearances. He recalled Manning mentioning them and that he suspected they were linked to the murders in some way.

"Of course, I've seen the way he is around you. He'll try to find you regardless, but he'll also send men to France to search for the prisoners, dividing his forces. It'll be almost too easy to take control of the communities in this country. With your power, I'll have their numbers decimated before he even realizes what's going on, and with any luck, he'll assume I've taken you to France and go there himself. Rowan will let me know as soon as he finds out.

"As for your incentives, you'll be glad to know that I, in fact, hold the prisoners in this country. Their lives are also contingent upon your obedience, as well as that of your sister. In no more than two days' time, you will submit to Antoine and release your power. Failing to do so will result in deaths, starting with your sister's."

The malicious grin Royce sent him was enough to make the bile churning in Quinn's stomach come up, but he held it back, along with the tears that threatened to fall. There had to be something else his father hadn't thought of. Some glitch in his reasoning that Manning would discover and use to his advantage, but Quinn could think of nothing. Except...

The cold vastness of despair rose swiftly to swallow him whole, but he refused to let it take him. One option still remained, one that had always been available, but that Quinn had never had the courage to take. That changed now. He owed that much to the people who'd accepted and loved him beyond measure. His only consolation was that Manning was still unbonded, and eventually he would find another mate. One that could give him the happiness he deserved.

* * * *

"Manning?"

Manning glanced back at the stranger tailing him but kept walking, anxious to get back to his mate. "Do I know you?"

"*Jaes'din.*"

That made him pause. Slowly, he turned his full attention on the man, taking in every minute detail of his visage and noticing for the first time his heavy French accent. Immediately, he was struck by the similarities between the stranger and his mate. Before him was the same black hair falling in shoulder-length waves and the same soft gray eyes staring from a pale, exquisitely formed face. The man was much taller, though, and broader of frame with a bearing that bespoke subtle authority. He was no shifter, however, and very few humans knew the *Ba'Kal* language. Fewer still who could identify him as the *Jaes'din* on sight.

Then the stranger tilted his head in the same fashion as Quinn, and Manning's hackles rose with a fury. "Are you the *Magnique*?" he asked, keeping his tone too low to be overheard by the humans rushing around them.

"No. I'm his...other son, Rowan. Call your men to you. We need to talk."

A veil of dread settled over him and he kept eyes trained on the man while pulling his cellphone from his back pocket. He pressed Cain's number on speed dial and waited for the man to pick up.

"Cain."

"Where is my mate?"

There was a whispered curse, then, "We're looking for him now. He's been gone about ten minutes."

A surge of rage swept through Manning so violent it turned his vision red. His mate was gone, and the man before him was apparently the only one who could give him answers. "Come to me. Now." He ended the call and returned the phone to his pocket. Even in the clustered terminal, his *Ketai* would be able to find him by scent. They arrived a few minutes later and, without saying a word, Rowan turned and led them to the elevators.

As soon as they stepped out into the underground parking garage, Manning grabbed Quinn's brother by the neck and slammed him into the nearest wall. "Talk, before I give in to the urge to rip your throat out."

"I wouldn't do that if I were you," a female called out.

Manning darted a glance at the petite woman approaching them. She had to be several centuries old, judging from the generous amount of silver hairs interspersed with dark brown. The locks were swept back into a severe bun, but her face held a timeless youth that softened the austerity of her chiseled features. Her clothes were surprisingly casual in comparison to the innate power Manning could feel emanating from her very being. Oddly, it reminded him of Merebeth and the way she could humble him at times with just her presence.

Manning looked back to Rowan and tightened the grip around his neck. Instead of fighting back, though, Rowan only kept his hands up, palms out, as if in surrender. "What have you done with Quinn?"

"I am very sorry about the death of your historian," the woman spoke again. "I felt her passing when it happened. She was a very dear friend of mine. My name is Xenessa, historian of the *Vam'kir*." When that garnered no response, she said, "You won't find Quinnten by choking the life out of his brother. We're here to help, and right now your mate needs you."

Manning glanced back to her knowing gaze. "How do you know he's my mate?"

"Merebeth told me. She also revealed to me the truth of his origin, and right now *Miel se Luuda's* dearest creation is in the hands of a man bent on the annihilation of your race. Let us help you get him back."

Manning narrowed his eyes. He could smell the truth in her words, but it still took every ounce of his willpower to release the neck in his grasp. "Tailor, get the car."

They waited in tense silence while Tailor ran to fulfill his order. Ten minutes later, they loaded into Manning's car with the historian in the passenger seat and Rowan securely seated between Manning and Cain in the back.

He reined in his temper and turned to Rowan. "So tell me something that won't result in your death."

The other man smiled grimly. "It's good to know my brother found a fitting mate. He deserves it after what I've discovered happened to him."

There was no sarcasm in his tone, but Manning kept his stone expression.

Rowan sighed and turned as much as he could to face Manning. "I'll tell you everything I know, but before I start, I have a proposition for you. I'll tell you where your mate is being taken if you swear upon a truce between your kind and mine."

Manning felt his lip curl in a snarl. "You'll tell me where my mate is in exchange for your life, trancer."

"My life is of little consequence unless we work together and free my brother. Do you really think my father will have a use for me if he convinces Quinnten to release his power? If I have to, I'll get my brother out myself, but I could use your help."

The man had a point, and Manning begrudgingly nodded for him to go on.

"I never knew what had happened to Quinnten. At the time of his...maturing, as your kind calls it, I was away conducting the affairs of my father. He wanted me trained and ready for the role I would take upon his relinquishment of the throne. When I came back to find my brother gone, my father told me he'd run away, and Mara would give me no more information than I already had. It was about six months ago when I was making the customary rounds to our clans that I discovered a small group of your kind being held prisoner at a camp nearby one of our clans."

"The disappearances," Cain murmured.

"So you're aware. I left to confront my father immediately—"

"And left them there?" Manning asked, disgust thick in his tone.

"I'll admit I have no love for your kind, shifter. Like you, I was raised on stories of the cruelty of my enemy, but even I couldn't stand by and allow the torture this lot was put through. Had I freed them, however, my father would have known it was me and either killed me himself or hired someone to do it for him. I was given the impression by the men holding them that they were merely the latest captives to be shipped from America under the orders of the *Magnique*. You have to understand that my hands were tied. My death would've solved nothing."

Manning gave another nod, a sliver of admiration piercing his hatred of the man sitting next to him. He'd never met a Vam'kir willing to stand up to the injustices of Ba'Kal captives, let alone one that would divulge this weakness to his enemy.

"When confronted, my father confided in me his plans to collect a horde of shifters to hold against you when he waged the war he was planning. I pretended to go along with it, swearing my loyalty and secrecy, and in return he has kept me aware of most of his proceedings. Again, understand that my true allegiance is to the survival of my race. If my father is allowed to continue with his plans, both sides will suffer, and that I will not have."

Rowan took a deep breath and turned his head. Manning thought he caught the faint scent of tears in the air before the evidence was shimmering before him in the man's eyes as he looked back.

"I knew my father was searching for something in particular when we came here a few weeks ago, but he wouldn't tell me what. I had no idea he planned to abduct my sister to use against Quinnten. Mara..." He swallowed heavily. "Mara told me everything in private after they brought her in. The truth about our brother, his relationship to you and how my father planned to use him as well as how he'd abused him in the past."

Rowan pinned him with a fierce stare. "She said my brother held out for four years, and I'm counting on him to hold out for a little longer. I want this to end, this needless bloodshed. I can tell that you love Quinnten, and from the fact that you haven't bonded with him yet—" At Manning's startled look, he shrugged. "I can smell it on you, or rather the lack of his blood running through your veins. That tells me you're not after him for the power he holds within.

"I want you to amass your forces and confront the army my father has flown in from France. Most of them are innocent men only following orders. Their lives need not be taken, but I need them to see what they're up against, and to know that we can form a truce instead of plunging into a war that could wipe out both of our races. I'll hold up my end of the bargain by killing my father before there is bloodshed. Once he's dead, I'll be the *Magnique* and have the power to force my men to stand down while you do the same for yours. Do we have an agreement? Be advised that I can smell a lie like a foul stench."

"As can I," Manning retorted, though his tone had lost its malice. Rowan was indeed telling the truth, from what he could sense, and as much as he hated to admit it, he felt a blooming respect for the man who was his enemy. "You have my word, on one condition."

Rowan lifted an elegant brow. "And that is?"

Manning grinned, feeling for the first time since meeting Quinn's brother, that he might be able to salvage his promise of safety to his mate after all.

* * * *

Quinn woke to the rough jostling of hands jerking him out of the limo. The cold night breeze sent a chill racing over his flesh as his limp body was thrown over a wide shoulder. Antoine's familiar odor filled his nostrils but, with the drug still running through his veins, he had no choice but to endure it. His head bobbed listlessly against the man's lower back as he was carried like a useless prize across an expanse of open pavement. The smell of gas wafted through the air, letting him know other vehicles were nearby, and the sounds of voices filled his hearing. They were numerous and growing louder as they neared their destination, mixed in with those of his father and Antoine's as a few began to call out inquiries while others welcomed their king back.

The ground changed to scuffed tile and from that to stairs. From his limited view, he saw they were in a large building of some sort and that it housed a great number of Royce's men judging by the scents of food and burning wood swirling around him. The air grew warmer as they ascended and the buzz of voices receded until they were almost nonexistent. After two flights of stairs, blue carpeting replaced the metal slats and they came to a stop at the end of a long hallway. A door creaked open and Antoine walked inside what seemed like a private room for its silence. Quinn heard the door close again with no other footsteps falling in their wake.

He wasn't prepared to be tossed onto a mattress and subsequently bit into his tongue as his head bounced. Blood filled his mouth and some trickled past his slack lips before he could swallow it. As the bed dipped under Antoine's weight, he felt hands tugging at his sneakers and socks. His pants were next, and the caress of skin on skin as his thighs were explored made his insides shrivel with revulsion. The hands traveled unerringly to his pelvis and skirted his genitals as though teasing him with perverse seduction. Knees pressed into his sides as he was straddled about the hips and the hard evidence of arousal dug into the muscles of his lower abdomen.

Antoine's square face appeared above him then, shadowed by the fall of dark auburn hair turned a muddy brown in the dim lighting. The curl of his upper lip reflected the sinister gleam in his ash brown eyes. When Quinn's head was cradled so that he was forced to look directly up at his tormentor's face, he poured all of his emotions into his narrowed gaze.

Pure loathing burned in every fiber of his being. How many times had he been paralyzed by the simple sound of this man's voice? Emasculated by the touch of his hands and the intent focus in his eyes? There was still fear, riddling holes through the confidence Quinn had worked so hard to attain, but he was no longer that naïve innocent his father had corrupted so long ago. Mara had taught him to fight, and Manning had given him the strength of will to face his fears. He would not let their efforts go to waste.

Antoine must have recognized his resolve, for he sat up and tilted his head to the side in studious contemplation. "I can see that your body isn't the only thing you've been working on, is it, boy? Have you forgotten all of your lessons?" He leaned forward to ghost his lips across the curve of Quinn's neck, his hot breath fanning the fine hairs just above Quinn's ear. "Or is this challenge I see your way of welcoming me back?" Antoine reared back and tore open the front of Quinn's shirt, extending his nails to scrape the flesh underneath.

Quinn clenched his eyes shut and swallowed convulsively against the pain. Tears pricked the back of his eyes but he blinked them away. He would not give the man the satisfaction of seeing his response.

"Antoine!"

His tormentor whipped his head around at the sharp crack of the *Magnique's* voice.

"He's no good to us until the drug wears off and we have more important matters to attend to at the moment."

"Sir, with all due respect—"

"Do not make me repeat myself." Royce's tone dripped with ice. "For four years you tried to break him and failed. You're lucky I'm giving you this chance to prove yourself worthy of ruling beneath me. Now come."

Antoine reluctantly climbed from the bed, but not before backhanding Quinn across the cheek, snapping his head to the side. Above the hammering of his heart, he listened to the sounds of their retreat until all that could be heard was the distant hum of activity two floors down.

Chapter Fifteen

Quinn had been taken in the late-morning, and judging from the cloak of darkness that had surrounded them on their way into the building, several more hours would pass before his system burned through the lingering effects of the drug. His mind wandered for a while to the years of his childhood, the days of simplicity when his mother had looked upon him with fondness, if not love, and his father had treated him with civility.

As the second son, he'd been considered superfluous, but never in the eyes of his siblings. Mara had always been his nurturing voice of reason, and Rowan... Rowan had been his hero, the older brother who could do no wrong. When had he changed, and what had their father done to bring it about?

Quinn veered his mind away from those circling thoughts, knowing they would only lead to grief. An image of Manning danced briefly in front of his vision, but he shut it away with ruthless determination. He couldn't think about what was forever lost to him, not in this place with the inevitable finality of his fate looming just hours away. His death was the only way to prevent the war his father was brewing, and if it had to come by his own hand, so be it.

And so he waited, drifting along the seams of time as it passed without measure.

His extremities were the first to regain mobility, and with effort he worked them as best he could, wriggling his fingers and toes then wrists and ankles to revive the vitality in his muscles. As soon as his arms and legs were once more under his control, he rolled himself off the bed and crawled to the bucket they'd provided him in the far corner of the room to relieve his screaming bladder. After he threw aside the tatters of his shirt, he sat stiffly against the wall and concentrated inwardly on his spirit. Its greeting to his call was lackluster and weak, but he hounded it with fierce doggedness.

Come on, buddy. It's just you and me now, and I need your help. But it remained impassive, still reeling from the inhibiting drug. Quinn gnashed his teeth in frustration. He stood on wobbly legs and walked over to the only window in the room, pulling back the heavy beige curtains to peer through the iron bars that caged it to the ground below. The hour of twilight marked the formation of shadows along the wide expanse of open land that ended with a line of forestry about a half mile away. He recalled the sleepless nights of the past when he would look out upon the darkness and see a pair of yellow orbs gleaming at him, assuring him he wasn't alone.

The memory sparked a feral response from his spirit and he felt it surge forth with renewed fortitude. It missed its golden-eyed panther, as much as Quinn missed Manning. A corner of Quinn's mouth quirked up in a smile. *Traitor. You always were on his side more than mine.* His spirit yawned flippantly, as though he were stating the obvious.

With a shake of his head, he walked back to the bed, hardening his heart with each step. He still had a part to play with no more time to waste. With extended nails, he cut narrow strips out of the threadbare sheet on the mattress and was about to tie them into a makeshift rope when the sound of boots scuffing along the carpet outside of the room made him freeze. Antoine's familiar odor preceded him and Quinn forced himself into action. He ripped away one of the strips and wrapped both ends around his fists then sprinted to the wall behind the door.

Seconds later, it opened to emit the large frame of his tormentor. Quinn steeled himself, tensing for the perfect opportunity. *Just a little farther, asshole. Just one more step. That's all I...* Antoine stepped fully into the room and Quinn leaped, tackling him from behind and looping the strip of cloth around his throat. The man went down with a thud and Quinn jammed his knee between Antoine's shoulder blades, pulling back with all of his strength, but it wasn't enough.

Antoine rolled over, forcing Quinn to scramble out of the way to keep from being crushed, and brought his fist back in a wide arc. The blow caught Quinn on his left temple and he fell to the floor in a daze. The man grasped him by the throat and yanked him up until his feet dangled above the floor.

"You worthless fool," Antoine spat out. "Is this how you honor your father? By forsaking all that he's done for you?"

Quinn struggled desperately then felt a moment of weightlessness as he was flung across the room. He hit the far wall with a sickening crack and he slumped to the floor, back throbbing in agony.

"He could've killed you the moment he realized the abomination you were," Antoine said as he advanced, "but he took mercy on you and kept you alive. You should be groveling at his feet in gratitude." He knelt and smacked Quinn hard across the mouth. "Before this day is over, I'll have you groveling at mine, because if you don't, it'll be your sister kneeling before me."

At the mention of his sister, rage tore through him with the violence of a hurricane. A deep growl formed in his chest that swiftly took on the timbre of a wild animal. His spirit clawed for dominance and initiated the change that melded their two souls into one. Quinn saw the terrified shock in Antoine's eyes right before he darted out from under the man and locked his canines onto the tendon just above the man's right heel. He shook his head savagely and felt a rush of triumph as the tendon gave way and a screeching howl rang in his ears.

Pain erupted along his side as razor-sharp nails sliced into his ribcage, the force of the swipe sending him skidding several feet across the floor, but he jumped back onto his padded feet. With a lunge, he crashed into Antoine's chest and angled his head at the last moment, sinking his teeth into the vulnerable flesh of the man's throat. Antoine thrashed furiously, raking his nails over the back of the fox, but Quinn only clamped on tighter, reveling in the hot, viscous fluid that spurted into his mouth and over his face. Great shudders racked the body beneath him as it sprawled on the floor, gurgling its protest as death lured it into a cold embrace.

Quinn couldn't move, couldn't think past the lust of the kill that vibrated through his being like pure, unbridled energy. It felt so good to let go and give in to the nature of his beast. Too good. There was no remorse or guilt in what he'd just done. He felt himself teetering on the edge of sanity, his animal side fighting for dominion. Finally, his conscience kicked into gear with the knowledge of who he was reminded of. Quinn's mind quickly shied away from the path of his thoughts. He was not his father, a soulless killer devoid of emotion.

The blood surrounding his maw began to coagulate and the stench became too much to bear. He unlocked his jaw and stumbled back, body shifting of its own accord as his stomach heaved and emptied its contents. Blood mixed with acid spewed from his mouth, and sweat broke out over his trembling body. Just as the uncontrollable racking ended, more footsteps sounded in the hall and he backed himself to the wall, eyes trained on the door standing slightly ajar.

A man came in, his features unrecognizable at first, and Quinn bared his fangs in challenge. Words were spoken in a soothing manner and hands rose in a gesture of peace but several seconds passed before Quinn's mind emerged from the haze that clouded it. Rowan's face, his voice and words slowly came into focus, and another tide of anger rolled through Quinn.

"It's just me, Quinnten. I'm not going to hurt you. It's all right now," Rowan was saying as he approached steadily.

Quinn snarled and sprang forward as soon as his brother was in striking distance. He punched Rowan in the jaw, throwing his entire body into it.

Rowan staggered to the side and rubbed his chin. "Okay, I guess I deserve that."

Quinn swung again, catching him in the nose this time. His brother stumbled back and pinched it while putting his other hand up to ward off further attack.

"Stop, damn it! I get the point. I'm an asshole. You want to hit me again or you want to go meet your mate?"

Quinn reared back a third time but paused as those words sank in. "My mate?"

Rowan swiped at the trails of blood leaking from his nose then lowered his hands. "Yeah. Manning's waiting outside." His gaze flicked to the body on the floor then back to Quinn, roaming in silent assessment. "I was too late," he murmured quietly. "*Sweet Mother*, this ends here. Tonight," he said with a curt whip of his hand.

"It will never end!" Quinn shouted, not caring if he was overheard. He wrapped his arms about his waist and took a step back. "Not unless I end it."

Despair crept in as the anger he'd been holding onto began to dissipate. His brother followed him and reached out a hand, but Quinn flinched away reflexively.

"I'm sorry, little brother. I should've been there for you, but you have to trust me now. Manning is outside with an army of shifters waiting just beyond the line of the woods. Xenessa can't mask their scents for long, so we need to hurry."

Quinn frowned. He could tell Rowan wasn't lying, but what he was saying didn't make any sense. "If he's out there, then why hasn't he attacked by now?"

Rowan's mouth lifted in a crooked grin. "Because he threatened to kick my ass if I didn't get you to safety first. We're going to do this without bloodshed, and without losing you. I swear it."

He stared at the other man for long seconds, afraid to hope, yet even more afraid to stay where he was. Finally, he nodded and watched as his brother stripped out of his light jacket and held out to him in offering, but he couldn't bring himself to take it. Rowan sighed and laid it on the foot of the bed. Only when he was to the door did Quinn pick the garment up and slide it on, wincing as the material scraped across his broken flesh. The jacket wasn't much, but the hem fell just past his groin, effectively covering his nudity. His brother began to lead him down the hallway outside, but Quinn stopped as he remembered his sister.

"Mara."

Rowan looked back in puzzlement. "She's here, but we'll have to come back for her later. It'll be over long before any harm can come to her."

Quinn shook his head resolutely. "We have to get her now. Father might use her as leverage." *Again.*

"Brother, she's safe where she —"

"Now!" he barked. In this he would not budge. He owed Mara his life, and if he had to find her himself, he'd do it.

A flash of irritation sparked in Rowan's eyes before it gave way to a hint of amusement. "You and your mate are a lot alike. Both of you have the same annoying streak of stubbornness. All right, let's do this." He continued down the hall and took one flight of stairs to the second floor. Another hallway, with the same worn carpeting running its length, followed. Halfway down, he took out a set of keys and inserted one, then pushed the door open as he stood aside.

Quinn entered hesitantly. The room was completely barren except for a huddled form in the far corner. Mara was wearing the same clothes he'd seen her in last, the mass of her raven hair falling like a shroud around her. She blinked up at him unseeingly with red-rimmed eyes, but Quinn could tell the moment they found clarity. She was in his arms in the next instant, squeezing so tightly he had to bite his tongue to keep from crying out. The pain paled in comparison, however, to the deep sobs that shook his sister's stately frame.

"She's alive. I promise Cassie's alive." He repeated those words over and over again until they penetrated the well of Mara's anguish. The tears streaming down her beautiful face as she pulled away and searched his eyes for the truth, wrenched at his heart. "She's alive," he said again, kissing her swollen lips.

"But we gotta go," Rowan called from the doorway.

Mara looked belatedly at their brother. "You kept your word."

Rowan nodded with a faint smile. Unfortunately, that didn't save his face. Mara strode over and punched him on the jaw, giving him a bruise to match the one on the other side.

"That's for taking so long," she said, stepping around him to head down the hallway as if nothing had happened.

A grin formed on Quinn's lips at his brother's sour expression, not an ounce of sympathy in him. They ran to the end of the hallway, where Rowan took out the keys again to open the last door. The room inside was the same size as the others, but was lavishly furnished. At the window on the other side, Rowan threw open the curtains and lifted the frame.

"Climb down the ladder but wait for me when you reach the ground."

Mara headed out first, gingerly reaching for the iron rungs of the ladder a foot to the left of the window and making her way down. Quinn followed next with his brother right above him. As soon as his feet touched the ground, he could feel it. The ebb and flow of energy that mirrored the bond he held with his spirit, only on such a grand scale as to make him pause in awe.

They were here. His kind.

Quinn wanted to laugh out loud but stifled it at the last moment. Joy filled his being at the knowledge that his mate was truly out there, hidden among the shadows of the trees. Then he realized just how close they were cutting it. The pale luster of dawn was beginning to crest over the horizon and though the *Vam'kir* historian was somehow masking the shifters' scents, she wouldn't be able to hide them once the sun's rays lightened the darkness of the forest in which they hid.

They raced across weeds and gravel to the side of the long building, stopping at its edge for Rowan to check around the corner. Quinn could hear the boisterous voices of the men and women his father had amassed to carry out his plans for genocide. The majority of them seemed to be outside at the front of the building, with his father's voice rising above theirs, shouting out indistinguishable words. Most likely giving a speech that painted portraits of victory in the minds of his followers.

Rowan waved his hand and started on the long stretch to the edge of the forest with Quinn hot on his heels, but they both stopped when they noticed the absence of Mara's light footfalls behind them. Quinn turned to see his sister crouched beside the brick wall, her body turned toward the commotion with fangs and nails extended. Dread tightened his chest as he realized what she was about to do.

"No, Mara no!"

But it was too late.

Mara used her preternatural speed to fly across the ground to the front of the building and toward the man responsible for the near death of her mate. Quinn ran after her with Rowan chasing behind, but he knew they wouldn't be able to reach her in time. She was going to be cut down before she even reached their father.

And he saw it as he rounded the next corner. Rowan grabbed him from behind and, before he could struggle out of his brother's grip, he watched in horror as the scene played out before him in agonizing detail. Mara was a black-and-white streak through the crowd of trancers gathered in front of the white-washed steps leading to the entrance of the building where their father stood. At the same time, a black shape burst from the trees a quarter mile away and sped across the open land like rippling fluid. The sleek form ate away the distance with the speed of a *Vam'kir*, yet Quinn knew it was a shifter. The energy of his mate drawing near was unmistakable.

A cry went out from the crowd and the guard standing nearest the *Magnique* raised a gun and aimed it at Mara as she leaped from the mass and charged the object of her fury. The shifter collided into his sister just as she was about to reach her target and the gun fired.

"No!" Quinn screamed. His body slipped from his brother's hold as he became one with his spirit and he took off in the direction of his mate. Chaos reigned all around him as more shifters joined the fray and violence broke out. He weaved through the moving cluster and lunged for the high porch. In the distance, another shot rang out, but his entire focus was on

Manning's unique scent and the stuttering beat of his failing heart.

Quinn caught sight of Manning in his human form lying prone on the porch with Mara kneeling beside him. Her gaze met Quinn's, eyes filled with horror and hands clamped around Manning's neck to staunch to pool of blood growing beneath him. Quinn scrambled toward them in fear until pain exploded in his side from a vicious kick. He flew through the air then slammed into the wall of the mansion. Agony ripped through him as his head bounced off the floorboards and the wounds on his side were torn open from the fall.

As his consciousness wavered, his spirit form receded in a rush, leaving him to his vulnerable human state. Before he could force his arms and legs to work, a hand wrapped around his throat and lifted him several feet above his full height. Another jarring slam into the side of the mansion had him reeling from the impact. When his vision finally came back into focus, he met the seething glare of his father. Rage spiked within Quinn and he fought to break loose from the man's grip but couldn't find purchase. His feet dangled above the porch and the hand around his neck was like iron.

Royce shouted at his men to keep the shifters at bay then turned back to Quinn. His upper lip curled in disgust. "I should've killed you a long time ago. You are no son of mine, only a traitor. I see the lust you have for that beast. Your own kind isn't good enough for you? Not even when it could mean our downfall?"

Quinn clawed helplessly at the hand choking off his air supply. The blood thrumming in his ears nearly drowned out Manning's fading heartbeat, dividing his concentration.

"Submit now," his father continued. "Redeem yourself and give us your power or I will let your precious beast die and mount his head on my blade for all his warriors to see."

It was no empty threat. Quinn had seen the same blood-crazed look in his father's eyes more than a few times. With proof of Manning's death, there was no telling whether the Ba'Kal warriors would choose to keep fighting without a leader or surrender. While Quinn highly doubted the second option, he also knew his father would kill Manning regardless of the outcome.

"Father!" Mara screamed in outrage.

Royce's hand only tightened around Quinn's throat. Quinn felt his resolve slipping as he stared out beyond his father to the battle raging on the mansion grounds. The congestion was so thick, he couldn't tell which side was winning. If he gave in to his father's demand, maybe he could convince the man to spare the warriors. If he didn't, their deaths could be certain. He knew Manning would want him to be strong, but there was too much on the line. Too many uncertainties.

"Magnique." Rowan's voice cut through the commotion and drew their attention instantly. He approached slowly from the side of the porch until he was within arms-reach, one hand kept subtly behind his back.

Royce grinned maddeningly. "It's about time you showed up. Take him while I kill their pathetic leader. We will finally put an end to this."

"I'm done taking your orders," Rowan said in a cold tone. "All my life, I've believed in your self-righteous sermons. That when the enemy kills one of us, they hurt us all. Yet, you would torture and sacrifice your own blood to commit genocide when not even the Ba'Kal would stoop so low. You are right about one thing, though. There is going to be an end to this."

Royce's face turned red in fury as he quickly realized the extent of his heir's betrayal. He grabbed the knife from the harness at his side but not fast enough. Rowan brought his hand out from behind his back in a backslash and sliced through the Magnique's throat with the hidden blade in his fist.

Blood spewed across Quinn's face before he fell to the porch and coughed spasmodically. With trembling hands, he swiped the warm fluid from his face and saw his father fall only a few feet away. Royce's face was frozen in a mask of death, his head partially decapitated and lolling to the side.

Rowan bent down and grabbed the Magnique's hair with one hand, the other poised with the blade just above the Magnique's body. "Go to your mate," Rowan said firmly. "You don't need to see this."

Shock and a sudden sense of gratitude flowed through Quinn. While he'd accepted his brother's change of heart to their father's loyalties, this was beyond what he could've hoped for. Rowan was not only taking charge, he was eliminating the Magnique's twisted scheme to gain power and implementing a new order. One that would force the Vam'kir to hold the Ba'Kal in regard by his act of defending them. At the same time, Rowan ran the risk of execution for the assassination of the Magnique. He was still young and without the full support of their kind to back him.

No. That won't happen, Quinn thought determinedly. Rowan was putting everything on the line to save him and the Ba'Kal. For that, he would have the full power of the *Aucinthe* behind him.

Fear rebounded through Quinn as he remembered the only way to help his brother was by bonding with Manning and releasing his power. He looked over to where Mara still held tight to Manning's neck in a desperate attempt to keep him alive and saw the anguish written on her face.

With a surge of panic, he raced to his mate and replaced Mara's hands with his own. Dread seized his mind as he saw that the bullet had grazed a vein. Blood spurted through his fingers despite the pressure he put on the wound.

"No. Nononono, please!" he cried. A soft caress flitted over his forearm and he looked into his mate's face to see stark love shining from his dark eyes. Manning's ashen lips moved, but no words came out. "No! You won't die."

Quinn leaned forward and clamped his mouth around the wound, drinking in the blood of his mate and releasing a deep moan, but whether it was from the intoxicating taste or the alarm of so much gushing down his throat, he wasn't sure. He sat up then and dropped his fangs, tearing into his wrist and pressing it to his mate's open mouth.

"Drink, damn you, drink!" This had to work. Bonding required sex, but there was no time for that. This had to be enough. It had to be.

He felt it then. A soft whisper fluttering along the very essence of his soul. It spoke of peace and radiated a consuming warmth that should have been calming, but it only made him fight harder. He knew what it was, could feel *Miel se Luuda's* soothing tendrils of energy wrapping around both him and Manning, but he wouldn't let her have him. Again, he bit into his wrist and pressed it to his mate's mouth.

"You can't have him!" he cried. "Not now." *I love him. Please don't take him.* Tears blurred his vision as he collapsed onto his mate and listened to the fading beat of his heart.

* * * *

Manning looked on with admiration and sorrow at the tall figure that stood with his back to the small group, as custom dictated. Adan would not turn around, nor wave goodbye, for his path lay before him, in the strong and welcoming arms of the Mother. But he would not leave yet, not until he felt the presence of his other son among those gathered to witness his passing.

The comforting scents of fresh rain and chocolate filled Manning's lungs and he turned to see his mate walking into the clearing with Mara. A small smile curved his lips as pride and love swelled in his chest, and the moisture on the tips of Quinn's lashes only increased the surge of his emotions. Manning held out a hand to his mate, who took it with a sad smile of his own. Together, with family and friends all around them, they watched the former *Jaes'din* shift to the large form of a golden hawk and take flight in a powerful thrust of black-tipped wings. The great warrior soared into the sky and circled once, gliding on the currents of the wind before heading north to meet his fate and rejoin his lost mate.

Manning closed his eyes and sent a silent thanks to the man who had been a stronger father than he'd ever needed to be. Because of his strength, Manning was able to look forward to the happiness he'd once only dreamed of.

When he opened his eyes again, it was to the sight of his mate staring up at him, love emanating from his unwavering gaze. He took Quinn's face into his hands and leaned down to lick at the tears gathered along the seam of his lips. The taste of Quinn's compassion burst along his taste buds and he delved deeper, swirling his tongue into the cavern of his mate's mouth and drinking in the soft moan that came out. The sound went straight to his groin and he wrapped an arm around the smaller man, pulling him close to feel the warmth of his body melting against his. Quinn's subtle arousal bloomed and infused itself into Manning's being, mixing with the rush of his desire and making his head spin with need.

Damn, he would never get enough of this, and he would never let it go, not even in death.

The gift of bonding *Miel se Luuda* had bestowed upon them in the midst of battle had twined their souls together, negating the powerful, lust-driven urges Quinn had previously incited in unmated Ba'Kal and Vam'kir. The bond also ensured they would follow each other into the afterlife when their time came. It was the most unorthodox bonding he'd ever heard of, but then, his mate wasn't exactly a man to be considered ordinary.

"Somebody pry the happy couple apart. This is killing me," Tailor grumbled as he walked past.

Quinn broke away laughing, wiping at the tracks of his tears. "You'll find your mate one day."

"Not before I do," Rowan smirked.

"You can't even shift yet," Tailor countered. "How are you going to deal with a mate?"

A round of laughter filled the clearing as they all headed back to the mansion. Manning felt a sliver of pity for the new *Magnique* who was muttering under his breath, but no more than that. He had his own problems to deal with, like the craving for blood that would hit him in a few days with the next full moon.

Quinn's power had been released when *Miel se Luuda* had bonded them, and whatever any of them had expected, it hadn't been what had occurred. Every *Ba'Kal* Alpha and Beta, along with their direct descendants, had taken on the inherent characteristics of the *Vam'kir* race, including the need for blood during the full moon. But even more astounding was the inclusion of certain *Vam'kir* in the doling out of power. Each clan leader, as well as their equivalent Betas and direct descendants, had been given spirits. Xenessa had speculated that it was *Miel se Luuda's* way of giving second birth to her firstborn race. Those who were now of both races would spread their seed through the bonding of mates until the two races were once more whole.

Though it was still in debate as to why the *Vam'kir* had been included when the history book stated that only the race of the *Aucinthe's* mate would prosper from his power, Manning had his own theory about that. And he was looking right at the reason, who was quickly becoming like a brother to him. He speculated it was Rowan's love for his race, proven when he'd killed his own father to ensure peace, that had enabled the *Vam'kir* and *Ba'Kal* to finally reach a truce and end a devastating war before it had even begun. The man had courage in spades, and Manning could think of no one better suited to lead his former enemy race into an age of peace.

He even forgave the man for arriving too late to save Quinn from Antoine, after he'd added a few more bruises to his pretty face.

"Speaking of mates, now that I've bonded with mine..." Mara paused to give the giggling blonde at her side a kiss, "I was thinking of settling down. You know... Have a few kids. What do you say, Manning?"

Manning glanced at her over the top of his mate's head with a frown. "Sounds good. You could adopt." He grunted as Quinn thumped him across the chest with the back of his hand.

Mara laughed. "Or I could be a surrogate mother." When no response came, she said, "And further the peace between our races." Manning frowned again and she threw her head back with a groan. "Quinn, smack him again. Knock some sense into your mate."

This time, Quinn's hand landed on the gut and Manning scowled down at his mate's wide-eyed look.

"She's offering to have your child," Quinn whispered, as though he were missing the obvious.

Manning froze in disbelief. Rowan clapped him shoulder on the other side and leaned in to say, "'Grats man, and by the way, don't say no. She gets ugly when she doesn't get her way." Cassie was bouncing with her usual enthusiasm and Quinn was staring at him with a smug grin.

"Are you serious?"

"No," Mara said with a wave of her hand. "Horrifying my brother-in-law is just something I like to do on the weekends. Of course I'm serious! So, are you going to answer?"

A wave of laughter bubbled up in his chest and he let it free. "Yes. Thank you."

The woman shrugged nonchalantly. "Well, you did save my life, but don't think I love you or nothin'."

"Manning, let me know when you're ready," Rowan said as they entered the mansion's backyard.

He nodded, knowing they still had to go over their plans for seeking out those of the abductees they hadn't found yet. Not all of the Vam'kir had conformed to Rowan's new order of peace. Those of Royce's men who had been charged with guarding the Ba'Kal prisoners were nowhere to be found. Thanks to Quinn, Manning and Rowan knew they were somewhere in the United States, though no more information had been gained on the matter. None of the Vam'kir who had submitted under the rule of the new Magnique had come forth with any clues. Manning still wasn't sure whether that was because those who'd been closest to Royce were lying or whether they truly didn't know anything.

But that could wait until later.

Manning slowed his gait enough to let the others pass them by before yanking on his mate's hand. As soon as Quinn turned with a frown, he took possession of the man's mouth. He plunged in as his mate's lips parted and guided his tongue in a slow dance of seduction. Quinn responded instantly by wrapping his arms around Manning's waist and pressing his budding erection against Manning's rigid length.

Quinn pulled away to look up, his eyes flashing green under the bright rays of the sun. "Have I told you lately how much I love you?"

Manning chuckled and kissed his mate again. "Every day."

And he did. Of course, Manning would always be chasing his fox, but he wouldn't have it any other way.

"Get a room," Cain called out from a distance.

"Get a life!" they yelled in unison.

About the Author

I have always been a lover of books, particularly those with the dichotomy of the strong alpha male and the weaker love of their life which they must rescue. After reading all I could find in M/F books, I decided to give M/M fiction a try and my addiction skyrocketed.

Hot, sexy men times two? No contest. Unfortunately, I was reading faster than the authors could produce. Eventually, I resorted to imagining my own stories and my mind took off from there.

I have to admit, though, I am a bit of a recluse. If not for the joy and humour my husband and four boys bring to me, I would never have ventured this far.

Nikki McCoy loves to hear from readers. You can find her contact information, website details and author profile page at http://www.totallybound.com.

Totally Bound Publishing

TOTALLY
BOUND
Home of Erotic Romance